G000292763

No Orchids for Miss Blandish

© 2013
Cover © CanStockPhoto/voronin76

Black Curtain Press
PO Box 632
Floyd VA 24091

ISBN 13: 978-1627551090

First Edition
10 9 8 7 6 5 4 3 2 1

CHAPTER ONE

1

It began on a summer afternoon in July, a month of intense heat, rainless skies and scorching, dust-laden winds.

At the junction of the Fort Scott and Nevada roads that cuts Highway 54, the trunk road from Pittsburgh to Kansas City, there stands a gas station and lunchroom bar: a shabby wooden structure with one gas pump, run by an elderly widower and his fat blonde daughter.

A dusty Lincoln pulled up by the lunchroom a few minutes after one o'clock. There were two men in the car: one of them was asleep.

The driver, Bailey, a short thickset man with a fleshy, brutal face, restless, uneasy black eyes and a thin white scar along the side of his jaw, got out of the car. His dusty, shabby suit was threadbare. His dirty shirt was frayed at the cuffs. He felt bad. He had been drinking heavily the previous night and the heat bothered him.

He paused to look at his sleeping companion, Old Sam, then shrugging, he went into the lunchroom, leaving Old Sam to snore in the car.

The blonde leaning over the counter smiled at him. She had big white teeth that reminded Bailey of piano keys. She was too fat to interest him. He didn't return her smile.

"Hello, mister," she said brightly. "Phew! Isn't it hot? I didn't sleep a wink last night."

"Scotch," Bailey said curtly. He pushed his hat to the back of his head and mopped his face with a filthy handkerchief.

She put a bottle of whiskey and a glass on the counter.

"You should have beer," she said, shaking her blonde curls at him. "Whiskey's no good to anyone in this heat."

"Give your mouth a rest," Bailey said.

He carried the bottle and the glass to a table in a corner and sat down.

The blonde grimaced, then she picked up a paperback and with an indifferent shrug, she began to read.

Bailey gave himself a long drink, then he leaned back in his chair. He was worried about money. If Riley couldn't dream up something fast, he thought, we'll have to bust a bank. He scowled uneasily. He didn't want to do that. There were too many Feds around for safety. He looked through the window at Old Sam, sleeping in the car. Bailey sneered at the sleeping man. Apart from being able to drive a car, he was useless, Bailey thought. He's too old for this racket. All he thinks about is where his next meal is coming from and sleeping. It's up to Riley or me to scratch up some money somehow—but how?

The whiskey made him hungry.

"Ham and eggs and hurry it up," he called to the blonde.

"Doesn't he want any?" the blonde asked, pointing through the window at Old Sam.

"Does he look like it?" Bailey said. "Hurry it up! I'm hungry."

He saw through the window a dusty Ford pull up and a fat, elderly man get out.

Heinie! Bailey said to himself. What's he doing here?

The fat man waddled into the lunchroom and waved to Bailey.

"Hi, pal," he said. "Long time no see. How are you?"

"Lousy," Bailey grunted. "This heat's killing me."

Heinie came over. He pulled out a chair and sat down. He was a leg man for a society rag that ran blackmail on the side. He was always picking up scraps of information, and often, for a consideration, he passed on any useful tips that might lead to a robbery to the small gangs operating around Kansas City.

"You can say that again," Heinie said, sniffing at the ham cooking. "I was out at Joplin last night covering a lousy wedding. I was nearly fried. Imagine having a wedding night in heat like this!" Seeing Bailey wasn't listening, he asked, "How's tricks? You look kinda low."

"I haven't had a break in weeks," Bailey said, dropping his cigarette butt on the floor. "Even the goddamn horses are running against me."

"You want a hot tip?" Heinie asked. He leaned forward, lowering his voice. "Pontiac is a cinch."

Bailey sneered.

"Pontiac? That nag's a fugitive from a merry-go-round."

"You're wrong," Heinie said. "They spent ten thousand bucks on that horse and it looks good."

"I'd look good if anyone spent all that dough on me," Bailey snarled.

The blonde came over with his plate of ham and eggs. Heinie sniffed at it as she put the plate on the table.

"Same for me, beautiful," he said, "and a beer."

She slapped away his exploring hand, smiled at him and went back to the counter.

"That's the kind of woman I like—value for money," Heinie said, looking after her. "Two rolled into one."

"I've got to get some dough, Heinie," Bailey said, his mouth full of food. "Any ideas?"

"Not a thing. If I do hear I'll let you know, but right now there's nothing your weight. I've got a big job tonight. I'm covering the Blandish shindig. It's only for twenty bucks, but the drinks will be free."

"Blandish? Who's he?"

"Where have you been living?" Heinie asked in disgust. "Blandish is one of the richest guys in the state. They say he's worth a hundred million."

Bailey speared the yolk of his egg with his fork.

"And I'm worth five bucks!" he said savagely. "That's life! What's he in the news for?"

"Not him: his daughter. Have you ever seen her? What a dish? I'd give ten years of my life for a roll in the hay with her."

Bailey wasn't interested.

"I know these rich girls. They don't know what they're here for."

"I bet she does," Heinie said and sighed. "Her old man's throwing a party for her: it's her twenty-fourth birthday—just the right age. He's giving her the family diamonds." He rolled his eyes. "What a necklace! They say it's worth fifty grand."

The blonde came over with his meal. She was careful to keep out of his reach. When she had gone, Heinie pulled up his chair and started to eat noisily. Bailey had finished. He sat back and began to pick his teeth with a match. He was thinking: fifty grand! I wonder if there's a chance of grabbing that necklace? I wonder if Riley would have the nerve to make a try for it?

"Where's the party—at her house?"

"That's right," Heinie said, shoveling food into his mouth. "Then she and her boy friend, Jerry MacGowan, are going on to the Golden Slipper."

"With the necklace?" Bailey asked casually.

"I bet once she puts it on, she'll never take it off."

"But you're not sure?"

"She'll be wearing it all right. The press will be there."

"What time will she be at the roadhouse?"

"Around midnight." Heinie paused, his fork near his mouth. "What's on your mind?"

"Nothing." Bailey looked at him, his fleshy face expressionless. "She and this guy, MacGowan? No one else?"

"No." Heinie suddenly laid down his fork. His fat face was worried. "Now look, don't go getting any ideas about the necklace. You'd start something you couldn't finish. I'm telling you. Riley and you aren't big enough to handle a job like that. You be patient. I'll find something you can handle, but not the Blandish necklace."

Bailey grinned at him. Heinie thought he looked like a wolf.

"Don't get excited," he said, "I know what I can and can't handle." He stood up. "I guess I'll be moving. Don't forget: if anything comes up, let me know. So long, pal."

"You're in a hurry all of a sudden, aren't you?" Heinie said, frowning up at Bailey.

"I want to get off before Old Sam wakes up. I'm not buying him another meal as long as I live. So long."

He went over to the blonde and paid his check, then he walked over to the Lincoln. The heat hit him like a clenched fist. After the whiskey it made him feel a little dizzy. He got in the car and paused to light a cigarette, his mind busy.

Once the word got around about the necklace, he was thinking, every little gangster in the district would sit up and wonder. Would Riley have the nerve to grab it?

He nudged Old Sam awake.

"Come on!" he said roughly. "What the hell's the matter with you? Don't you do anything but sleep these days?"

Old Sam, tall, wiry and pushing sixty, blinked as he slowly straightened up.

"Are we going to eat?" he asked hopefully.

"I've eaten," Bailey said and set the car moving.

"How about me?"

"Go ahead if you've got any dough. I'm not paying," Bailey snarled.

Old Sam sighed. He tightened his belt and pushed his greasy, battered hat over his long, red nose.

"What's gone wrong with this outfit, Bailey?" he asked mournfully. "We never have any money now. One time we were doing all right; now nothing. Know what I think? I think Riley spends too much time in the sack with that broad of his. He isn't concentrating on business."

Bailey slowed the car and pulled up outside a drugstore.

"Give your mouth a rest," he said and getting out of the car, he walked into the drugstore. He shut himself in a telephone booth. He dialed, and after a long wait, Riley came on the line.

Bailey could hear the radio blaring and Anna singing at the top of her voice. He started to tell Riley what he had learned from Heinie, but gave up.

"You can't hear what I'm saying, can you?" he bawled. "Can't you stop that goddamn noise?"

Riley seemed half dead. Bailey had left him in bed with Anna. He was surprised he even bothered to answer the telephone.

"Hang on," Riley said.

The music stopped, then Anna began to shout angrily. Bailey heard Riley bellow something and then the sound of a loud smack, Bailey shook his head, breathing hard down his nose. Riley and Anna fought all day. They drove him nuts when he was with them.

Riley came back to the telephone.

"Listen, Frankie," Bailey pleaded. "I'm roasting alive in this goddamn booth. Will you listen? This is important"

Riley began to beef about the heat at his end.

"I know: I know." Bailey snarled. "Will you listen? We've got the chance of grabbing a necklace worth fifty grand. The Blandish girl will be wearing the necklace tonight. She's going to the Golden Slipper with her boy friend— just the two of them. I got the word from Heinie. It's the McCoy. What do you say?"

"How much?"

"Fifty grand. Blandish—the millionaire. How about it?"

Riley seemed to come alive all of a sudden.

"What are you waiting there for? Come on back!" he said excitedly. "This is something we got to talk about. Come on back!"

"I'm on my way," Bailey said and hung up. He paused to light a cigarette. His hands were shaking with excitement Riley wasn't as yellow as he thought, he said to himself. If we handle this right, we're in the money!

He walked with quick strides back to the Lincoln.

Old Sam looked at him sleepily.

"Wake up, stupid," Bailey said. "Things are cooking."

2

Bailey moved self-consciously around the outer fringe of the tables in the main restaurant of the Golden Slipper. He was glad the lights were dim. Although Anna had washed his shirt and cleaned up his suit, he knew he still looked like a bum and he was worried someone would spot him and throw him out.

The roadhouse was crowded and doing a roaring business. The staff was too busy to notice him. He got in a dark corner where he had a general view of the big room and leaned against the wall.

The noise of voices struggling to get above the sound of the band deafened him. He kept looking at his watch. The time was ten minutes to twelve. He looked around the room. Over by the main entrance, three or four photographers stood waiting with flash cameras. He guessed they were waiting for the Blandish girl. He had never seen her and knew he wouldn't be able to recognize her so he watched the photographers.

It was like Riley to play the big shot and make him go into the club while Riley sat outside with Old Sam in the Lincoln, Bailey thought. He was always getting the dirty end of the stick. Well, when they split the money, he would quit the gang. He had had about enough of Riley and Anna. With the money he'd get from the diamonds, he would buy himself a chicken farm. He had come from a farming family and if he hadn't got into trouble and had to serve a three year stretch he wouldn't have ever teamed up with Riley.

His thoughts were suddenly interrupted by the band breaking off and going into their hot version of "Happy Birthday to You."

Here she comes, Bailey thought and raised himself on his toes to look over the heads of the crowd. Everyone had stopped dancing and were looking towards the entrance. The photographers were shoving each other, maneuvering for better positions.

A bright spotlight suddenly went on as Miss Blandish made her appearance, followed by a tall, handsome man in a tuxedo.

Bailey had only eyes for Miss Blandish. He sucked in his bream sharply at the sight of her. The hard light caught her red-gold hair and reflected back on her white skin. He thought he had never seen such a beautiful girl. She wasn't like any of the girls he knew. She had everything they had and then a lot more. He watched her wave gaily to the crowd who stamped and shouted around her. He stood tense, staring at her, and he didn't relax until the row had died down and she had seated herself with MacGowan at a distant table.

He had been so impressed with the girl's beauty that he had forgotten the necklace, but now, as he got over the first impact of her loveliness, he saw the necklace and again his breath sucked in between his clenched teeth.

This splendid collar of flashing diamonds brought him out in an excited sweat. Looking at them, he suddenly realised what a commotion there would be when they were stolen. This was going to be the big take, he thought. Every cop in the country would be after them. Maybe he had been crazy to have encouraged Riley to grab it, he thought, wiping his sweating hands. Blandish had millions and he would raise hell. Once they had that necklace, the heat would be fierce.

Bailey looked across at Miss Blandish's table. He noticed that MacGowan was flushed. He seemed to be drinking steadily, and once when he refilled his glass, Miss Blandish put her hand on his as if trying to persuade him to stop drinking. MacGowan just grinned at her, emptied his glass, then getting up took her out onto the dance floor.

That bird's getting stiff, Bailey thought. If he goes on drinking like that, he'll be out on his feet.

The crowd was getting rowdy. Everyone seemed half drunk.

Bailey sneered at them. Have enough money, he thought, bitterly, and you behave like hogs.

He caught sight of Miss Blandish being jostled in the crowd. She suddenly broke away from MacGowan and made her way back to the table. MacGowan followed, protesting. They sat down. MacGowan began to drink again.

At a table near where Bailey stood, a blonde girl was quarreling with her escort, a fat, elderly man who looked pretty drunk. The blonde suddenly got to her feet, lifted a bottle of champagne out of its bucket and poured the contents of the bottle over her escort's head. He sat there, gaping at her, the champagne soaking his white tuxedo and plastering down his hair.

The blonde put the bottle back into the bucket and sat down again. She blew a kiss to the fat man. The people near them had all turned to stare. Some of the men were laughing. The fat man got slowly to his feet. His red face was tight with rage. He threw the contents of his soup plate in the girl's face. She began to scream frantically. A youngish man jumped to his feet and punched the fat man who staggered back and cannoned into the table behind him, upsetting it with a crash of glass and china. The two women at the table jumped up, screaming.

Hogs! Bailey thought. He looked across the room at Miss Blandish. She was standing, shaking MacGowan's arm impatiently. MacGowan got unsteadily to his feet. He followed her to the exit.

The girl who had had the soup thrown in her face was still screaming. A fight had developed between two drunks and the youngish man. The struggling men surged up to Bailey and hindered him from following Miss Blandish. He punched his way clear, sending the men staggering, then walked quickly to the exit.

He passed MacGowan leaning against the wall in the lobby, waiting for Miss Blandish. He ran down the drive to the waiting Lincoln. Old Sam was at the wheel and Riley sat by his side.

"They'll be out in a minute," Bailey said, getting in behind Riley. "She'll be driving. Her boy friend is stewed to the gills."

"Get going," Riley said to Old Sam. "We'll stop at that farm we passed coming. We'll overtake her after she has passed us and crowd her off the road."

Old Sam put it into gear and the Lincoln slid away. Bailey lit a cigarette and took his gun from his shoulder-holster. He laid the gun on the seat beside him.

"She got the diamonds?" Riley asked.

"Yeah."

Riley was taller and thinner than Bailey. He was five or six years younger. But for the cast in his right eye, he wouldn't have been bad looking, but the cast gave him a shifty, sly look.

Old Sam drove fast for half a mile, then coming to the farm, he slowed down, ran the car onto the grass and pulled up.

Riley said, "Get out and watch for her."

Bailey took his gun, tossed his cigarette away and got out of the car. He stood by the side of the road. In the distance, he could see the lights of the roadhouse and he could hear the faint sound of the band playing. He waited for several minutes, then he saw the headlights of an approaching car.

He ran back to the Lincoln.

"Here they come."

As he got into the car, Old Sam started the engine. A two-seater Jaguar swept past. Miss Blandish was driving. MacGowan seemed to have passed out.

"Get going," Riley said. "That's a fast job. Don't let them get away."

The Lincoln stormed after the Jaguar.

It was a dark, moonless night. Old Sam turned on hi? headlights. The beams lit up the Jaguar. They could see MacGowan's head rolling with the motion of the car.

"He wont start trouble," Bailey said. "He's had a real skinful."

Riley grunted.

The next bend in the road brought them to wooded country. At this hour the road was completely deserted.

"Okay," Riley said. "Now crowd her!"

The needle of the speedometer moved to eighty-five and then to eighty-eight. The Lincoln held the road without any roll. The wind began to whistle and the trees took on a smudged look. The distance between the two cars remained the same.

"What are you playing at?" Riley said, staring at Old Sam. "I said crowd her!"

Old Sam shoved the gas pedal to the boards. The Lincoln

crept up a few yards, but the Jaguar surged forward and the distance widened.

"She's too fast for this crate," Old Sam said. "We're not going to catch her."

The cars were now traveling at over eighty miles an hour. The Jaguar was steadily pulling away.

Suddenly Old Sam saw his chance as they approached a fork in the road.

"Hang on!" he yelled, slammed on his brakes and flung the wheel over. The tires screamed on the tar and the Lincoln spun around, skidding into the rough. Bailey was thrown off the rear seat. He felt the Lincoln lurch, then the off-wheels rise and slam back on the road. The car shuddered as Old Sam released the brakes and stepped down hard on the gas. He crashed over the grass verge, bumped and banged crazily across the rough ground and shot onto the road again.

By cutting off the corner, he was now in front of the Jaguar.

Bailey scrambled back on the seat, swearing and groping for his gun.

"Nice work," Riley said, leaning out of the car to look back.

Old Sam, watching the Jaguar in his driving mirror, began to zigzag about the road, slowing down and forcing the Jaguar to slow down. Finally the two cars stopped. As Bailey jumped out of the Lincoln, Miss Blandish began to turn the Jaguar. He reached her just in time. He leaned into the car, snapped off the ignition, then threatened her with the gun.

"Get out!" he shouted. "This is a stick-up."

Miss Blandish stared up at him. Her large eyes were wide with shock. MacGowan opened his eyes, and slowly sat up.

Riley, watching, remained in the Lincoln. He leaned out of the window, his sweating hand on his gun. Old Sam nervously opened the car door, ready to get out.

"Come on! Come on!" Bailey snarled. "Get out!"

Miss Blandish got out of the car. She didn't look frightened, but she was startled.

"What is all this?" MacGowan mumbled. He got out of the car, wincing and holding his head.

"Take it easy," Bailey said, threatening MacGowan with the gun. "This is a stick-up."

MacGowan sobered. He moved closer to Miss Blandish.

"Hand over the necklace, sister," Bailey said. "Quick!"

Miss Blandish's hands flew to her throat. She began to back away.

Bailey cursed. He was beginning to lose his nerve. A car might pass any moment, and then they would be in trouble.

"Hand it over or you'll get hurt," he snarled.

As she still backed away, he strode up to her with three quick strides. He had to pass close to MacGowan who suddenly came alive and slammed a punch at Bailey's head.

Bailey staggered, lost his balance and fell heavily. His gun slipped from his hand.

Miss Blandish stifled a scream. Riley didn't move. He thought Bailey could handle it. He didn't want either Miss Blandish or MacGowan to be able to identify him if the thing turned sour. He told Old Sam to watch the girl.

Old Sam shuffled over to Miss Blandish. She didn't seem to notice him. She was staring at Bailey who was up on one knee, cursing and shaking his head. Old Sam stood by her sheepishly, but he was ready to grab her if she tried to get away.

Bailey looked at MacGowan who came forward unsteadily, still drunk, but full of fight.

Bailey was up to meet him. He hit MacGowan on the side of his neck. It wasn't a good punch and it scarcely stopped MacGowan who slammed in a right to Bailey's stomach. Bailey grunted and went down on his knees. This punk certainly could punch. Why didn't Riley come? Before he could get up MacGowan had hit him on the side of the head and Bailey rolled on the grass.

Cursing, Riley got out of the car.

Bailey's hand touched his gun. He grabbed it, then as MacGowan moved towards him, he lifted the gun and pulled the trigger.

The bang of the gun made Miss Blandish scream. She covered her eyes.

MacGowan clutched at his chest, then he fell in the road. Blood showed on his white shirt.

Bailey got to his feet as Riley ran up.

"You crazy sonofabitch!" Riley snarled. He bent over MacGowan, then he looked up at Bailey who had come closer and was staring down at MacGowan, his face slack with fright.

"He's dead! You jackass! What did you kill him for? Now you have started something."

Bailey hooked his finger in his collar and jerked at it savagely.

"Why didn't you help me?" he mumbled. "What else could I have done? It wasn't my fault."

"Tell that to the judge," Riley snarled. He was badly scared. This is a murder rap now, he was thinking. We'll all burn. If they catch us...

Bailey looked at Miss Blandish who was staring at MacGowan's body. He said to Riley, "We'll have to knock her off. She knows too much."

"Shut up!" Riley said. He was staring at Miss Blandish. An idea had suddenly dropped into his mind. Here was a chance of getting into the real money. This girl's father was worth millions. He would pay anything to get her back safe. "She's coming with us."

Miss Blandish suddenly broke free from Old Sam. She spun around and began to run down the road. Cursing, Riley ran after her. She heard him coming and she began to scream. He caught up with her, grabbed her arm and as she turned, he hit her hard on the side of her jaw. He caught her as she slumped forward. Picking her up, he carried her to the Lincoln and bundled her in on the back seat.

Bailey came up.

"Now wait a minute..."

Riley turned on him, snarling. He grabbed Bailey by the front of his shirt.

"Keep out of this!" he raved. "You've landed us in a murder rap! If they catch us, we'll all burn. From now on, you do what I tell you! Get his body off the road and the car out of sight! Hear me?"

The viciousness in his voice startled Bailey. He hesitated, then as Riley released him, he went back to where Old Sam stood like a pole-axed bull.

He made Old Sam help him put MacGowan's body in the Jaguar, then he drove the car off the road into the wood.

The two men came running back to the Lincoln.

"You're nuts to snatch this girl," Bailey said as he got in beside Old Sam. "We'll have the Feds after us. How long do you imagine we'll last?"

"Shut up!" Riley said violently. "Now you've killed that guy, we daren't sell the necklace. Where do you imagine we'll get money from unless it's from Blandish? He's worth millions. He'll pay anything for the girl. It's our only chance. Now, shut up!" To Old Sam, he said, "Get moving. We'll go to Johnny's place. He'll hide us."

"Are you sure you know what you're doing?" Old Sam asked as he started the car.

"We've got nothing to lose thanks to this sonofabitch," Riley said. "I know what I'm doing. Get going."

As the car gathered speed, Riley turned to where Miss Blandish lay slumped in the corner of the car. He took the necklace from around her neck.

"Got a light?" he asked Bailey.

Bailey took a flashlight from his pocket and turned it on. Riley examined the diamonds in the beam of the flashlight.

"They sure are something," he said, awe in his voice. "But I'm not going to try to sell them. If Blandish wants them back, he'll have to pay for them. It'll be safer that way."

Bailey shifted the light so it played on Miss Blandish. She was still unconscious. In spite of the dark bruise on her face where Riley had hit her, Bailey thought she was the most beautiful woman he had ever seen.

"Some dish!" he said, speaking his thoughts aloud. "Is she all right?"

Riley looked at the unconscious girl. His eyes hardened.

"She's all right," he said. He stared at Bailey. "And for the record, she's going to stay all right so don't go getting any ideas about her."

Bailey turned off the flashlight.

The car roared on into the darkness.

3

A mile outside La Cygne, Old Sam said, "We want gas."

"Why the hell didn't you fill up before we set out?" Riley demanded violently.

"How was I to know we were going to Johnny's?" Old Sam whined.

Bailey turned his flashlight on Miss Blandish. She was still unconscious.

"She'll be okay," he said. "There's a gas station just ahead."

At the next bend in the road they saw the lights of the gas station. Old Sam pulled up by the pumps. A boy came out of the office, rubbing his eyes and yawning. He started to fill the tank. Riley leaned forward, screening Miss Blandish from him. He needn't have bothered. The boy was half silly with sleep. He didn't once look into the car.

Suddenly the lights of a car appeared around the bend in the road. A big black Buick pulled up close to the Lincoln. The arrival of this car startled the three men. Bailey dropped his hand on his gun.

There were two men in the Buick. The passenger got out. He was a tall, heavily built man with a black snap brim hat pulled low over his eyes. He looked with sharp interest at the Lincoln. He spotted Bailey's quick movement and he came over.

"You nervous or something?" he asked in a hard, aggressive voice as he stared intently at Bailey.

It was dark and none of the men could see each other distinctly.

Riley said, "Beat it, fella, nothing's biting nobody."

The big man peered in his direction.

"That sounds like Frankie," he said and laughed. "For a moment I thought it was some big shot shooting his mouth off."

The three men in the Lincoln stiffened. They looked across at the Buick. The driver had turned on the dash light so they could see him. He was covering them with a shotgun.

"Is that you, Eddie?" Riley said, his mouth turning dry.

"Yeah," the tall man said. "Flynn's nursing the cannon so don't start anything you can't finish."

"We're not starting anything," Riley said hurriedly. He cursed their luck to have run into one of the Grisson gang. "I didn't recognize you."

Eddie shook a cigarette from his pack and struck a match. Riley hurriedly moved his body to screen Miss Blandish but Eddie saw her.

"Some babe," he said, lighting his cigarette.

"We've got to get going," Riley said hurriedly. "See you sometime. Get going, Sam."

Eddie rested his hand on the car door.

"Who is she, Riley?"

"She isn't anyone you know. She's a friend of mine."

"Is that a fact? She seems unnaturally quiet."

"She's drunk," Riley snarled, sweat running down his face.

"You don't say!" Eddie pretended to be shocked. "I bet I can guess who made her drunk. Let's have a closer look at her."

Riley hesitated. Out of the corner of his eye, he saw Flynn get out of the Buick; the shot gun pointed directly at him. Reluctantly, Riley leaned back. Eddie took out a powerful flashlight and shone the beam onto the unconscious girl.

"Very nice," he said appreciatively. "You ought to be ashamed, Riley, making a nice girl like that tight. Does her ma know where she is?" He stepped back, blowing tobacco smoke into Riley's face. "Where are you taking her?"

"Home," Riley said. "Let's skip the comedy, Eddie. We've got to get moving."

"Sure," Eddie said, stepping further back. "I wouldn't be in her shoes to wake up and find myself with a car load of monkeys like you three. Beat it."

Old Sam let in the clutch and the Lincoln shot out into the highway. It went off down the road with ever-increasing speed.

Eddie watched them go. He took off his hat and scratched his head. Flynn put the shotgun back into the car and came over. He was a little man with a thin pointed face that made him look like a ferocious rat.

"What do you make of that?" Eddie asked, puzzled. "Something's in the wind."

Flynn shrugged his shoulders.

"We should care."

"You mean you should care," Eddie said, "but then you haven't my brains. What were those cheap mugs doing with a babe like that? Who is she?"

Flynn lit a cigarette. He wasn't interested. They had driven up from Pittsburgh and he was tired. He wanted to go to bed.

Eddie went on, "She's been socked in the jaw. Don't tell me a small timer like Riley has snatched her. I can't believe he'd have the nerve. I'm going to have a word with Ma."

"Oh, for Christ's sake!" Flynn grumbled. "I want some sleep tonight even if you don't."

Eddie ignored him. He went over to the boy who had been staring, his eyes round with fright.

"Where's your telephone?"

The boy led him into the office.

"Okay, buddy, go rest your ears outside," Eddie said as he sat on the desk. When the boy had gone, he dialed a number and waited. After a delay Doc's voice boomed over the line.

"I'm talking from the filling station outside La Cygne." Eddie said, speaking fast and keeping his voice low. "Riley and his mob have just pulled out. They had a girl with them: high class stuff and I mean just that. She's way out of their class. Riley said she was drunk, but she looked as if she'd been socked on the jaw. It's my guess Riley's snatched her. Tell Ma, will you?"

Doc said, "Hold on." After a long delay, he came back on the line. "Ma wants to know what she looks like and how she was dressed."

"She's a redhead," Eddie said. "She was more than pretty: better looking than most movie stars. I've never seen a better looking girl. She had one of those long, thin, aristocratic noses and a high forehead. She was wearing a white evening dress and a black wrap, and they cost plenty."

He could hear Doc talking to Ma and he waited impatiently.

"Ma thinks it might be the Blandish girl," Doc said, coming on the line. "She was going to the Golden Slipper out at Pine Valley tonight and she was wearing the Blandish necklace. I can't imagine Riley going for a job that big, can you?"

Eddie's mind worked fast.

"Ma could be right. I thought there was something familiar about the girl. I've seen pictures of the Blandish girl and come to think of it, this girl looks like her. If Riley's got her and the diamonds—he's got plenty."

Suddenly Ma's harsh violent voice came over the line. "Is that you, Eddie? I'm sending the boys down right away. Meet them at Lone Tree junction. If Riley's got the Blandish girl, he'll take her to Johnny's place. There's no place else for him to take her. If it's the girl, bring her back here."

Eddie said, "Anything you say, Ma. How about Riley's gang?"

"Do I have to tell you everything?" Ma snarled. "Use your head and get going!"

The line went dead.

Eddie hurried out to the Buick. He gave the boy a dollar, then he got into the car beside Flynn.

"Let's go," he said, his voice excited. "Ma is sending the boys to meet us. She thinks Riley has snatched the Blandish girl!"

Flynn groaned.

"She's nuts. Those cheap hoods wouldn't have the nerve to snatch a purse let alone the Blandish dame! Where are we going, anyway?"

"Lone Tree junction, then on to Johnny's place."

"Goodbye sleep," Flynn said savagely. "That's close on a hundred goddamn miles." He sent the car moving onto the highway.

Eddie laughed.

"You can sleep anytime," he said. "I want another look at that babe. Get going!"

Flynn shoved the gas pedal to the boards.

"That's all you think about—women!"

"What else is better to think of?" Eddie asked. "It's women and money that make the world go round."

4

Dawn was breaking over the hills as the Lincoln climbed the long steep hill that led to Johnny's hide-out.

Old Sam drove carefully. He was tired, but he didn't want to admit it. He was always scared these days that Riley would get rid of him for being too old. Bailey and Riley kept looking through the rear window of the car to make sure no one was following them. They were both nervous and their tempers were short.

Miss Blandish sat as far away as she could from Riley. She had no idea where she was being taken. None of the three men had spoken to her since she had recovered consciousness. She was frightened to draw attention to herself by asking questions. She was sure that by now her father would have alerted the police and they would be looking for her. It could be, she tried to assure herself, only a matter of time before she was found, but in the meantime, what was going to happen to her? This was a thought that kept intruding into her mind, filling her with dread. She had no illusions about these men who were with her. She could see how frightened they were. The two younger men, she thought, were the ones to beware of.

During the long drive, Riley could think of nothing but the menace of the Grisson gang. He was sure that Eddie would tell Ma Grisson about the girl. Ma was the smartest and most dangerous member of the gang. He was sure she would guess who the girl was. She would know about the diamonds too. What would she do? The chances were she would send her gang after them. Would she guess they were going to Johnny's place? He doubted this. Johnny only worked with the small timers. A gang as big as the Grisson gang wouldn't have dealings with a rummy like Johnny.

He would have to work fast, he told himself. As soon as he had got the girl under cover, he must contact Blandish. The quicker he got the money and the girl back to Blandish the safer it would be for him.

Old Sam swung the Lincoln onto the narrow dirt road that led directly to Johnny's place. He reduced speed, and after driving a mile or so, they came upon Johnny's shack, a two-storied wooden building, screened by trees. Leading to it was a rough path that had been cut through the undergrowth.

Old Sam pulled up and Bailey got out.

"See if he's around," Riley said, staying where he was. He fingered his gun, looking nervously at the undergrowth.

Bailey went over to the shack and hammered on the door.

"Hey, Johnny!" he shouted.

There was a pause, then Johnny opened the door. He looked at them suspiciously.

Johnny was pushing seventy. He was a tall, skinny old man with a drink-sodden face and dim, watery eyes. At one time, years ago, he had been one of the best safe men in the business, but drink had ruined him.

He looked at Bailey, then over at the car. His eyes took in Miss Blandish.

"What is it?" he asked. "You boys in trouble? It's Bailey, isn't it?"

Bailey tried to crowd into the shack, but Johnny stood firm.

"We want to stay here for a few days, Johnny," Bailey said.

"Let us in!"

"Who's the girl?" Johnny asked not moving.

Riley pushed Miss Blandish out of the car and, followed by Old Sam, came over.

"Come on, Johnny, don't act coy," Riley said. "Let us in. There's plenty of dough in this for you. Come on; don't keep us out here."

Johnny stepped back and Riley shoved Miss Blandish into the shack that consisted of one large living room and two rooms upstairs leading out onto a wooden balcony that overhung the living room.

The living room was indescribably dirty. There was a table and four boxes to serve as chairs, an old cooking stove, a hurricane lantern hanging on the wall, a radio on a shelf and not much else.

Old Sam was the last to enter. He closed the door and leaned against it.

Miss Blandish ran over to Johnny. She caught hold of his arm.

"Please help me!" she said breathlessly. The smell of drink and stale sweat that came from him made her feel ill. "These men have kidnapped me. My father..."

Riley dragged her away.

"Shut up!" he snarled at her. "One more word from you and you'll get hurt."

Johnny was looking uneasily at Riley.

"I'm not getting mixed up in a snatch," he said feebly.

"Please telephone my father..." Miss Blandish began when Riley stepped up to her and smacked her face. She reeled back with a startled cry.

"I told you, didn't I?" he shouted. "Shut up!"

She put her hand to her face, her eyes flashing.

"You beast!" she exclaimed. "How dare you touch me!"

"I'll do more than touch you if you don't pipe down!" Riley snarled. "Sit down and shut up or I'll slap you again!" Old Sam came over. He looked worried. He picked up one of the boxes and put it close to Miss Blandish.

"Take it easy, miss," he said. "You don't want to upset the fella."

Miss Blandish sank onto the box. She hid her face in her

hands.

"Who is she?" Johnny asked.

"The Blandish girl," Riley said. "She's worth a million bucks, Johnny. We'll split even among the lot of us. We'll only be here three or four days."

Johnny squinted at him.

"Blandish—he's pretty rich, isn't he?"

"He's worth millions. How about it, Johnny?"

"Well..." Johnny scratched his dirty scalp. "I guess, but not for longer than four days."

"Where can I put her?" Riley asked. "Have you got a room for her?"

Johnny pointed to one of the doors leading off the balcony.

"Up there."

Riley turned to Miss Blandish.

"Get up there!"

"Do what he tells you, miss," Old Sam said. "You don't want any trouble."

The girl got to her feet. She went up the stairs. Riley followed her. On the overhanging balcony, she paused to look down at the three men who stared up at her.

Casually, Johnny walked over to the gun rack by the front door. There were two shotguns in the rack.

Riley kicked open the door of the room Johnny had indicated.

"Get in!"

She entered the small dark room. Riley followed her. He lit an oil lamp hanging from the ceiling and glanced around.

There was a bed with a dirty mattress, but no bedding. A jug of water with a thin film of dust floating on the water stood on the floor. A tin basin rested on a small packing case. Thick sacking was nailed across the window. There was a musty smell of damp in the room.

"This'll make a change for you," Riley sneered, "It'll take some of the starch out of you. Stay here and keep quiet or I'll come up and fix you."

Miss Blandish was watching a large squat spider crawling across the wall. Her eyes were wide with horror.

"Scare you?" Riley said. He reached out and picked the spider off the wall. The short hairy legs of the insect waved wildly. "Do you want me to drop it down your pretty dress?"

Miss Blandish backed away, shuddering.

"You behave yourself and you'll be all right," Riley said, grinning at her. "Start trouble and you'll be sorry." While he was speaking he was pinching the spider between his finger and thumb. "If you don't behave, I'll treat you the same way. Now you keep quiet."

He went out, shutting the door behind him.

Bailey and Old Sam were sitting on boxes, smoking. Riley came down the stairs.

"How about some food, Johnny?" he asked, then he stiffened.

Johnny was holding a shotgun in his hands, covering the three men. Riley's hand moved to his gun, but the look in Johnny's dim eyes stopped him.

"Don't start anything, Riley," Johnny said. "This gun'll blow your chest to pieces."

"What's the idea?" Riley asked through stiff lips.

"I don't like any of this," Johnny said. "Sit down. I want to talk to you."

Riley sat down near Bailey.

"It was on the radio half an hour before you arrived. Who killed the guy?"

"He did," Riley said, jerking his thumb at Bailey. "The stupid bastard lost his head."

"Like hell I did!" Bailey snarled. "I had to kill him. This rat let me handle him alone..."

"Oh, shut up!" Riley said violently. "What's it matter? The guy's dead and we have a murder rap around our necks but we've got the girl. If we can get the money from her old man, we have nothing to worry about."

Johnny shook his head. After hesitating, he lowered the gun.

"I've known you boys since you were kids," he said. "I never thought you'd turn killers. I don't like it. Murder and kidnapping. You'll have the Feds after you. You're going to get hot. You'll be public enemies. You are way out of your class."

"Your share of the loot will be two hundred and fifty grand," Riley said quietly. "That's big money, Johnny."

"Think of the booze you'll be able to buy with all that

dough," Bailey said brutally. "You'll be able to swim in whiskey."

Johnny blinked.

"There isn't that much money in the world."

"Two hundred and fifty grand, Johnny: all for you."

Slowly, Johnny put the gun back in the rack. The three men relaxed. They watched him collect some tin mugs and a big earthenware jar.

"You boys want a drink?"

"What is it?" Riley asked suspiciously. "Your own rot-gut?"

"It's good stuff—the best."

Johnny poured the applejack into the mugs and handed them around.

They drank cautiously. Bailey gagged, but Riley and Old Sam managed to get the burning stuff down their throats.

"How about some grub, Johnny?" Old Sam asked as he wiped his mouth on his sleeve. "I'm starving."

"Help yourself," Johnny said. "There's the pot on the stove."

As Old Sam went over to the stove, Bailey said to Riley, "You were wrong to snatch the girl. We should have killed her. Eddie will tell Ma Grisson and she'll send Slim after us."

"Shut up!" Riley yelled furiously.

Johnny stiffened.

"What's that? Slim? He isn't in this, is he?" he said.

"He's talking through the back of his head," Riley said.

"Yeah?" Bailey said. He looked at Johnny. "We ran into Eddie Schultz on the road. He saw the girl. He'll tell Ma Grisson."

"If Slim's coming in on this, I'm keeping out," Johnny said, edging towards the gun rack.

Riley pulled his .38.

Keep away from that gun! I'm not scared of Slim Grisson. He won't bother us."

"Slim's bad," Johnny said uneasily. "I know all you boys. I know when there's any good in you. There isn't any good in Slim Grisson. He's mean and bad right through."

Riley spat at the stove.

"He's got a hole in his head," he said. "He's no better than an idiot."

"Maybe, but he's a killer. He kills with a knife. I don t like guys who use a knife."

"Give it a rest," Riley said. "Let's eat."

Old Sam was serving stew onto tin plates.

"This stuff smells like goddamn cat," he grumbled. He spooned some of the mess onto a plate. "I'll take it up to the girl. She ought to eat."

"It won't suit her fancy taste," Riley said, grinning.

"It's better than nothing," Old Sam said.

He carried the plate up the stairs and he entered the dimly lit little room.

Miss Blandish was sitting on the edge of the bed. She had been crying. She looked up as Old Sam came in.

"Here, get this inside you," he said awkwardly. "You'll feel better for some grub."

The gamy smell of the stew turned Miss Blandish sick.

"No... thank you. I—I couldn't..."

"It stinks a bit," Old Sam said apologetically, "but you should eat." He put the plate down. He looked at the dirty mattress and shook his head. "Not what you're used to, I bet. I'll see if I can find you a rug or something."

"Thank you; you're kind." She hesitated, then lowering her voice, she went on, "Won't you help me? If you will telephone my father and tell him where I am, you will be well rewarded. Please help me."

"I can't, miss," Old Sam said, backing to the door. "I'm too old for trouble. Those two down there are mean boys. There's nothing I can do for you." He went out, shutting the door after him.

Riley and Bailey were eating and Old Sam joined them. When they had finished, Riley got up.

"That's about the worst meal I've ever eaten," he said. He looked at his watch. The time was five minutes after nine. "I'd better call Anna. She'll be wondering what's happened to me."

"You're kidding yourself," Bailey said. "You and your Anna. Do you imagine she cares where you are?" He got up and went over to the window.

Riley gave the operator Anna's number. After a delay, she came on the line.

"Hi, baby," he said. "This is Frankie."

"Frankie!" Anna's voice was strident. The three men could hear her. "Where have you been, you bastard? What do you think you're doing—walking out on me? How do you imagine I liked sleeping on my own last night? Where are you? What have you been doing? If you've been sleeping with some other woman, I'll kill you!"

Riley grinned. It was good to hear Anna's voice again.

"Take it easy, sweetheart," he said. "I've pulled a job— the biggest ever, and it's going to land us in the money. From now on, you're going to wear mink, baby. I'll give you so much dough you'll make that Hutton dame look like a pauper. Now, listen, I'm at Johnny's place—the other side of Lone Tree junction..."

"Riley!" Bailey's voice was high pitched with fear. "They're coming! Two cars—it's the Grisson gang"

Riley slammed the receiver back on its hook and rushed to the window.

Two cars had pulled up near the Lincoln. From it spilled a number of men. They started towards the shack. Riley recognized the tall, heavily built Eddie Schultz.

He spun around.

"Go up and stay with her," he said to Johnny. "See she doesn't make a sound. We've got to bluff these birds. Snap it up!"

He shoved Johnny up the stairs, and together they entered Miss Blandish's room. She was lying on the bed and she started up as they came in.

"There's a guy out there who's poison to you," Riley said, his face wet with the sweat of fear. "If you know what's good for you, stay quiet. I'm going to try to bluff him, but if he once gets the idea you're up here, you might just as well say your prayers—there's nothing else you can do."

It wasn't the words that sent a cold chill to her heart, it was the white circle of fear around his mouth, and the lurking terror in his eyes.

5

Riley stood on the balcony and looked down at the group of men who in turn stared up at him. Eddie was there, both hands sunk in his pockets, his black hat pulled down low. Flynn was standing on the extreme left of the group, his hands also hidden, his eyes cold and watchful. Woppy and Doc Williams stood by the door; both of them were smoking.

But it was Slim Grisson who held Riley's attention. Slim sat on the edge of the table. He was staring blankly at the tips of his dirty shoes. He was tall, reedy and pasty-faced. His loose, half-open mouth, his vacant, glassy eyes made him look idiotic, but a ruthless, inhuman spirit hid behind the idiot's mask.

Slim Grisson's background was typical of a pathological killer. He had always been lazy at school, refusing to take the least interest in book work. He began early to want money. He was sadistic and several times he had been caught torturing animals. By the time he was eighteen, he had begun to develop homicidal tendencies. By then, his mental equipment had degenerated. There were times when he would be normal to the point of being quick-witted, but most times he behaved like an idiot.

His mother, Ma Grisson, refused to believe there was anything wrong with him. She got him a job in a poolroom, cleaning glasses. Here he mixed with a bootleg mob. He watched them handle guns and wads of dollar bills. He got hold of a gun. His first killing followed automatically. He went on the run and for two years his mother lost sight of him. Then he returned. He boasted of the men he had murdered during the time he had lived alone. Ma Grisson was determined he should become a gang leader. She took his education in hand herself. Before he did a job, she coached him, going over every detail with him again and again. It was like teaching a monkey to do tricks. Once he got what she wanted into his head, he didn't forget. Ma got together several desperate men. There was Flynn just out after serving a four year stretch for robbing a bank. There was Eddie Schultz, one time bodyguard of one of the bosses of Murder Incorporated. There was Woppy, a clever safecracker, and Doc Williams, an old man who had been struck off the register and who was glad to be employed.

Over these men, she placed her son. They accepted him as their leader although it was Ma who was the power behind his throne. Without her he would have been helpless.

Riley was terrified of this reedy creature. He hung his hands on his coat lapels as a token of surrender. He stood motionless, looking down at the men below.

"Hi, Frankie," Eddie said. "I bet you're surprised to see me again."

Riley came slowly down the stairs. His eyes never left the group waiting for him.

"Hello," he said, his voice husky. "Yeah, I didn't expect to see you so soon."

He stood near Bailey who didn't look at him.

"Where's the gorgeous chick you had with you?" Eddie asked.

Riley made a tremendous effort to pull himself together. If they were going to get out of this jam with their skins, he had to bluff these men and bluff them convincingly.

"You didn't come all this way to see her again, did you?" he said, trying to sound at ease. "You weren't thinking of making a date with her, were you? That'd be too bad. We got tired of her company and ditched her."

Eddie tossed his cigarette on the floor and put his foot on it.

"Yeah? You don't say. I wanted another look at her. Who was she, Frankie?"

"Oh, just a broad," Riley said. "No one you'd know."

He was aware that all the Grisson gang, except Slim were staring at him with cold, bleak eyes. He had a sinking feeling they knew he was lying. The only one who paid him no attention was Slim.

Eddie said, "You didn't happen to pick her up at the Golden Slipper roadhouse, did you?"

Riley's belly suddenly felt cold and empty.

"That little chiseler? She wouldn't go to a joint like that. We picked her up at Izzy's bar. She was stewed so we took her for a ride and a little fun." Riley forced a smile that looked like a grimace. "But she wouldn't play so we let her walk home."

Eddie laughed. He was enjoying himself.

"Yeah? You should write for the movies, Frankie: you sure got an imagination."

Very slowly, Slim raised his head. He looked directly at Riley who flinched.

"Where's Johnny?" Slim asked.

"Upstairs," Riley said, feeling sweat running down his back.

Slowly Slim turned his head to look at Eddie. All his movements were deliberate.

"Get him," he said.

The door above opened and Johnny came onto the balcony. He leaned on the rail. The men below stared up at him.

Johnny didn't make enemies, nor did he take sides. He was strictly neutral.

Riley implored his silence with a long, meaning stare, but Johnny wasn't looking at him. He was looking at Slim.

Slim rubbed the side of his thin nose.

"Hello, Johnny," he said.

"Hello, Slim," Johnny said, keeping his hands on the rail, well in sight.

"Haven't seen you for a long time, have I?" Slim said with a smirking grin. His hands were on the move all the time. They moved up and down his thighs. They fingered his string tie. They straightened his shabby coat. They were restless, bony, frightening hands. "I've got a new knife, Johnny."

Johnny shifted his weight from one foot to the other.

"Good for you," he said and glanced uneasily at Eddie.

Slim made a sudden move. It was too fast for Johnny to follow. A knife suddenly appeared in Slim's hand. It was a thin bladed knife about six inches long with a black handle.

"Look at it, Johnny," Slim said, turning the knife in his hand.

"You're a lucky guy to have a knife like that," Johnny said, his face stiff.

Slim nodded.

"Yeah, I know. Look how it shines," The light from the sun, coming through the dirty window, reflected from the knife onto the ceiling. It made a dancing white pattern overhead. "And it's sharp, Johnny."

Doc Williams who had been standing a little behind Eddie, nervously chewing a cigar, moved forward.

"Take it easy, Slim," he said in a soothing voice. He recognized the danger signals.

"Shut up!" Slim snarled at him, his slack face suddenly vicious. His eyes Crawled up to where Johnny stood, motionless. "Come down here, Johnny."

"What do you want?" Johnny asked hoarsely without moving.

Slim started to dig his knife into the table.

"Come down here!" he said, slightly raising his voice.

Doc signaled to Eddie who said, "Leave him alone, Slim. Johnny is a pal of yours. He's a good guy."

Slim looked over at Riley.

"But he isn't such a good guy, is he?"

Riley sagged at the knees. The sweat glistened on his face.

"Let him alone," Eddie said roughly. "Put that sticker away. I want to talk to Johnny."

Eddie was the only member of the gang who could handle Slim in his bad spells, but Eddie was smart enough to know that he was dealing with explosive material. One day, he wouldn't be able to handle Slim.

Slim grimaced, then the knife disappeared. He looked sideways at Eddie and then began to pick his nose.

"We're interested in Riley's girl friend, Johnny," Eddie said. "Have you seen her?"

Johnny licked his dry lips. He wanted a drink. He wanted all these men out of his home.

"I wouldn't know if she's his girl friend," he said, "but she's in there."

No one moved. Riley drew in a sudden short breath and Bailey turned a whitish green.

"Let's see her, Johnny," Eddie said.

Johnny turned and opened the door. He called and then stood aside. Miss Blandish came out onto the balcony. The men stared up at her. When she saw them, she started back and shrank against the wall.

Woppy, Eddie and Flynn suddenly had their guns in their hands.

"Get their guns," Slim said, staring up at Miss Blandish.

"Go ahead, Doc," Eddie said. "We'll cover you."

Moving gingerly, Doc went over to Bailey and jerked his gun from the shoulder holster. Bailey just stood there, licking his lips. Then Doc got Riley's gun. As he turned, Old Sam suddenly went for his gun. He was surprisingly quick. The heavy gun boomed as Woppy shot him through the head. Doc felt the slug fan his face. He stepped back with a startled grunt as Old Sam spread out on the floor.

Riley and Bailey became livid. They stopped breathing for seconds.

Slim looked at them and then at Old Sam's body. He had a starved, wolfish look on his face. Johnny pushed Miss Blandish, sobbing hysterically, back into the bedroom.

"Get him out of here," Slim said.

Doc and Woppy dragged Old Sam's body out of the shack. They came back quickly.

Eddie walked up to Riley and dug him in the chest with his gun.

"Okay, chum," he said, biting off each word, "the act s over. You're in a fix. Spill it. Who's the girl?"

"I don't know," Riley gasped, his body shivering.

"If you don't, I do," Eddie said. He took hold of Riley's shirt front with his left hand and gently jerked him to and fro. "She's the Blandish girl. You snatched her to get the diamonds. We're on to you, sucker. You have the diamonds on you right now." He felt inside Riley's coat pocket and fished out the necklace.

There was a long silence while everyone stared at the necklace. Then Eddie released Riley.

"I'm sorry for you, sucker," he said as if he meant it. "I can't see any future for you."

He went over to Slim and gave him the necklace.

Slim held the necklace in the sunlight. He was entranced.

"Look Doc," he said. "Aren't they pretty? Look how they glitter. They're like stars against a black sky."

"They're worth a fortune," Doc said, staring at the necklace.

Slim's eyes went to the upstairs bedroom door.

"Bring her down here, Eddie," he said. "I want to talk to her."

Eddie looked at Doc who shook his head.

"How's about these punks, Slim?" Eddie said. "We've got to get back to Ma. She's waiting."

Slim was staring at the necklace.

"Get her, Eddie," he said.

Eddie shrugged. He went up the stairs. Johnny didn't meet his eyes as he went past him into the bedroom. Miss Blandish was leaning against the wall. She was trembling violently. When Eddie came into the room, her hand flew to her mouth and she looked around wildly for a way of escape.

Eddie felt sorry for her. He thought, even scared, she was the most beautiful girl he had ever seen.

"You don't have to be frightened of me," he said. "Slim wants you. Now listen, kid, Slim's not only mean, but he's not right in his head. If you do exactly what he tells you, he won't hurt you. Don't get him sore. He's as dangerous as a snake, so watch it. Come on: he's waiting."

Miss Blandish crouched back. Her eyes were dark with terror.

"Don't make me go down there," she said unsteadily. "I can't bear any more. Please let me stay up here."

Eddie took hold of her arm gently.

"I'll be with you," he said. "You've got to come. You'll be okay. If he starts anything, I'll fix him. Come on now, kid."

He brought her down the stairs.

Slim watched her as she came.

"She looks like she's come out of a picture book, doesn't she?" he mumbled to Doc. "Look at her pretty hair."

Doc was worried. He had never seen Slim in this mood before. Usually he hated women.

Eddie stood Miss Blandish in front of Slim. He stepped back, watching. Everyone watched.

Miss Blandish stared in horror at Slim who smiled at her, putting his head on one side, his yellow eyes glittering.

"I'm Grisson," he said. "You can call me Slim." He rubbed the side of his nose with his thumb. "These belong to you, don't they?" He held up the necklace.

Miss Blandish nodded. There was something so repulsive and terrifying about this creature that she had a mad urge to scream and keep on screaming.

Slim fingered the stones.

"They're pretty, like you."

He held them out. At the movement, Miss Blandish started back, shuddering.

"I'm not going to hurt you," Slim said, shaking his head. "I like you. Here, you take them. They belong to you. Put them on. I want to see what you look like with them on."

Eddie said, "Look, cut it out, Slim. That necklace belongs to all of us."

Slim giggled. He winked at Miss Blandish.

"Hear him talk? He wouldn't have the nerve to take them from me. He's scared of me—they're all scared of me." He held out the necklace. "Here, put it on. Let me see it on you."

Slowly, as if hypnotized, she took the necklace from him. The touch of the diamonds seemed to jolt her. With a gasping scream, she dropped the necklace and ran blindly up the stairs to where Johnny stood.

"Get me out of here!" she screamed frantically. "I can't bear any more! Don't let him come near me!"

She startled Slim. He stiffened and his knife jumped into his hand. From a weak-looking idiot he suddenly changed into a vicious killer. Half crouching, he faced the others.

"What the hell are you waiting for?" he screamed. "Take them out of here! Hurry! Get them out—get them out!"

Woppy and Flynn closed in on Riley and Bailey. They shoved them out of the shack and into the open.

Slim turned to Doc.

"Rope them to a tree!"

His face pale, Doc picked up some lengths of rope lying amongst a pile of rubbish in a corner. He followed Woppy and Flynn.

Slim looked at Eddie. His yellow eyes seemed on fire.

"Watch her. Don't let her get away."

He snatched up the necklace, dropped it into his pocket and went out into the hot sunshine. He was shaking with excitement. The urge to kill had taken possession of him.

He could hear Riley yammering hysterically. He could see his livid, glistening face and the way his mouth worked in terror.

Bailey walked silently. His face was pale, but dangerous lights smouldered in his eyes.

The group of men reached a small clearing in the thicket and, all realizing that this was the place of execution, they stopped.

Slim pointed to convenient trees.

"Tie them there," he said.

While Flynn covered Bailey, Woppy fastened Riley to the tree with the cord Doc tossed to him. Riley made no effort to save himself. He stood against the tree, shuddering, helpless in his terror. Woppy turned to Bailey. "Get up against that tree," he said savagely.

Bailey walked deliberately to the tree and set his back against it. As Woppy came up, he kicked like a snake striking.

His shoe sank into Woppy's groin, and then Bailey was behind the tree, the slim trunk between him and Flynn's gun.

Slim became violently excited.

"Don't shoot!" he screamed out. "I want him alive!"

Woppy writhed on the grass, trying to get his breath back. No one bothered about him. Doc stepped behind some bushes. His face was white and he looked sick. He was going to keep out of it.

Flynn slowly began to edge towards the tree while Slim stood motionless, the thin-bladed knife glittering in his hand.

Bailey looked around for a way of escape. Behind him the shrubs were thick; in front of him, Flynn approached cautiously; on his left, Slim stood with his knife. It was to his right that he must make his bid for freedom. He made a sudden dive, but Flynn was closer than he realised. He aimed a blow at Flynn who ducked. Bailey's fist went over Flynn's head and he floundered. Flynn closed with him.

For a minute they strained. Then Bailey who was the more powerful man, broke away. He slammed Flynn on the jaw and Flynn went down and out.

Bailey sprang away.

Slim hadn't moved. He stood there, his thin body drooping, his loose mouth half open and the knife hanging limply in his fingers. Woppy was still out. Bailey suddenly changed his ideas. There was only Slim. Doc didn't count. If he could knock Slim out, then he and Riley could surprise Eddie. It was worth the risk. He moved towards Slim who waited with yellow, gleaming eyes.

Then Bailey suddenly saw Slim grin. The idiot mask slipped and the killer was there. Bailey knew he was but a few heart beats from death. He had never felt so frightened. He stood still, like a hypnotized rabbit.

The knife flashed through the air and sped at him. He took the blade in his throat.

Slim stood over him while he died, watching and feeling the same odd ecstasy run through him which a killing always gave him.

Woppy had sat up, his face ashen. He began to curse softly. Flynn, still on his back, moved uneasily, a livid bruise growing on his jaw. Doc turned away. He wasn't callous like the others.

Slim looked over at Riley who shut his eyes. A horrible croaking sound came from him. Slim cleaned his knife by driving it into the ground. Then he straightened.

"Riley..." he said softly.

Riley opened his eyes.

"Don't kill me, Slim," he panted. "Gimme a break! Don't kill me!"

Slim grinned. Then moving slowly through the patch of sunlight, he approached the cringing man.

CHAPTER TWO

1

Miss Blandish was pushed into the hard light of the overhead lamp. Two pads of cotton-wool were strapped across her eyes with adhesive tape. Eddie supported her. She leaned heavily against him. His hand on her arm felt hard and warm. It was her only contact in the darkness.

From her chair, Ma Grisson stared at Miss Blandish. Before leaving Johnny's place, Eddie had telephoned her, telling her they were on their way. She had had time to appreciate what this kidnapping would mean to her and the gang. Handled carefully and with any reasonable luck, she and the gang would be worth a million dollars before the end of the week. For the past three years, she had built up the reputation of the gang. They hadn't made a great deal of money, but they hadn't done badly. They were regarded by the other gangs as good third-raters. Now, because of this slim, red-haired girl they would become the richest, the most powerful and the most wanted public enemies of Kansas City.

Ma Grisson was big, grossly fat and lumpy. Flesh hung in two loose sacks either side of her chin. Her crinkly hair was dyed a hard, dull black. Her little eyes were glittering and as impersonal as glass. Her big floppy chest sparkled with cheap jewelry. She wore a dirty cream colored lace dress. Her huge arms, mottled with veins, bulged through the lace network like dough compressed in a sieve. Physically she was as powerful as a man. She was a hideous old woman, and every member of the gang, including Slim, was afraid of her.

Eddie whipped the tape from Miss Blandish's eyes. It was a shock to her to be confronted by this old woman, sitting slumped in the armchair. At the sight of her, Miss Blandish caught her breath sharply and shrank back.

Eddie put his hand on her arm assuringly.

"Well, Ma," he said. "Here she is, delivered as per your instructions. Meet Miss Blandish."

Ma leaned forward. Her staring, beady eyes terrified the girl.

Ma hated talking as much as she hated talkers. She said one word when most people said ten, but this was an occasion she felt called for a speech.

"Listen to me," she said, "you may be Blandish's daughter but you mean nothing to me. You're staying here until your old man buys you back. It depends on him how long you do stay here. While you're here, you're going to behave. So long as you do behave, you'll be left alone, but if you start making trouble, you'll have me to reckon with, I promise you. You'll be sorry if you do cross me. Do you understand?"

Miss Blandish stared at her as if she couldn't believe this terrifying old woman really existed.

"Do you understand?" Ma repeated.

Eddie nudged Miss Blandish.

"Yes," she said.

"Take her up to the front room," Ma said to Eddie. "It's all ready for her. Lock her in and come down here. I want to talk to you."

Eddie led Miss Blandish from the room. As they went up the stairs, he said, "The old girl wasn't fooling, baby. She's meaner than Slim, so watch your step."

Miss Blandish didn't say anything. She seemed crushed and terrified.

A few minutes later, Eddie joined Doc and Flynn in Ma's room. Woppy had been sent downtown for news.

Eddie poured himself a shot of whiskey, then sat on the arm of a chair.

"Where's Slim got to, Ma?"

"He's gone to bed," Ma said. "Never mind about him. I want to talk to you and Flynn. You heard what I said to the girl about making trouble? The same applies to you two. Neither of you nor Woppy are going to start trouble just because there's a good-looking girl here. If I catch any of you interfering with her, you'll be sorry. More gangs have come to grief through a woman than through the cops. I won't have you boys fighting over her. That girl is to be left alone. Is that understood?"

Eddie grinned jeeringly.

"That go for Slim too?"

"Slim doesn't bother with women," Ma said, glaring at

Eddie. "He's got too much sense. If you thought more of your job and less about your cheap floozies, you would be better off. That also applies to Woppy and to you," she looked at Flynn who moved uncomfortably. "You understand? You're to leave the girl alone."

"I'm not deaf," Flynn said sulkily.

"And you, Eddie?"

"I heard you the first time, Ma."

"Okay." Ma reached for a cigarette and lit it. "This girl is worth a million dollars to us. She has been missing since midnight. By now Blandish will have alerted the cops and they will have alerted the Feds. We've got to contact Blandish and tell him to call off the Feds and get a million dollars in used bills ready for delivery. We shouldn't have any trouble with him. He has the money and he wants his daughter back," She looked at Eddie. "Go downtown and telephone Blandish. Tell him he'll get instructions soon how he is to deliver the money. Warn him if he tries to double-cross us, his daughter will suffer. I don't have to tell you what to say: make it raw and crude."

"Sure, Ma," Eddie said.

"Then get off."

As Eddie rose to his feet, he asked, "What's the split going to be, Ma? I'm the guy who spotted the girl. I ought to get more than the rest."

"We haven't got it yet," Ma said curtly. "We'll talk about it when we do get it."

"And how about me?" Flynn put in. "I was there too."

"Yeah?" Eddie answered. "If it hadn't been for me you would have gone to bed."

"Shut up!" Ma snapped. "Get off!"

Eddie hesitated, then meeting the hard little eyes, he shrugged and left the room. They heard the Buick start up and drive away.

"Now, you," Ma said to Flynn. "Who knows we're connected with Riley and his gang and with what happened last night?"

Flynn scratched his head.

"Well, there's Johnny, of course. He saw what happened and he knows we took the girl, but Johnny's okay. He's burying the three stiffs and getting rid of their car. We'll have to do something for him, Ma. Riley promised him a quarter share. The old fella expects us to see him right."

"We'll see him right," Ma said, "Who else is there?"

Flynn thought for a moment.

"There's the boy at the filling station. He saw Eddie talking to Riley. I guess he saw I had a gun. Maybe he even saw the girl."

"No one else?"

"No."

"I'm not taking any chances. Take care of the boy. He might talk. Get going."

When Flynn had gone, Ma settled more comfortably in her chair. She was aware that Doc Williams was prowling restlessly around the room and seemed uneasy. She looked questioningly at him. Her relations with him were on a different level from those of the rest of the gang. He was a man of education and that was something she respected.

She knew some years ago, Doc Williams had been a successful surgeon. He had been married to a woman twenty years younger than himself. She had suddenly gone off with his chauffeur and he had taken to the bottle. A few months later, while drunk, he had attempted a brain operation and the patient had died. He was tried for manslaughter and drew five years. He was struck off the register. Flynn had met him in prison and had brought him to Ma when they came out. Ma had been smart enough to realize the advantage of having a brilliant surgeon and doctor attached to the gang. From then on, she didn't have to worry about finding a doctor if any of her boys got shot. She kept Doc supplied with liquor and he looked after her boys.

"Handled right," Ma said, "we're in a safe position. I'm going to pass the word around that Riley snatched this girl. Sooner or later, the word will reach the cops. They'll look for him and when they find he's missing, they'll be sure he snatched the girl." She grinned, showing her large false teeth. "So long as they don't dig them up, they'll go on thinking they snatched the girl and we'll be in the clear."

Doc sat down. He lit a cigar. His movements were slow. His drink raddled face was worried.

"I don't like kidnapping," he said. "It's a cruel, horrible business. I'm sorry for the girl and her father. I don't like it."

Ma smiled. Doc was the only member of the gang allowed

to speak his mind or offer advice. Ma seldom took his advice, but she liked to listen to him. He was someone to talk to when she was lonely, and sometimes his advice was sound.

"You're a soft old fool," she said contemptuously. "The girl has had everything up to now. Let her suffer. Her old man's worth millions. He can afford to suffer too. I've suffered: so have you. Suffering does people good."

"Yes," Doc said. He poured himself a stiff drink. "But she is young and beautiful. It is such a waste of a young life. You don't intend to send her back to her father?"

"No, she isn't going back. When the money is paid, we'll have to get rid of her. She knows too much."

Doc shifted uneasily.

"I don't like it, but I suppose it's not my business." He emptied his glass and refilled it. "This is a big thing, Ma. I don't like any of it."

"You'll like the money when you get your share," Ma said cynically.

Doc stared at his glass.

"It's a long time now since I got excited about money. There's something I want to tell you. Slim behaved very oddly with the girl: very oddly indeed."

Ma looked sharply at him.

"What do you mean?"

"I was under the impression that Slim had no use for women. You told me that, didn't you?"

"Yes, and I'm glad of it," Ma said. "I've had enough trouble with him without having that kind of trouble."

"He's interested in this girl," Doc said quietly. "I've never seen him act the way he acted when he set eyes on her. He seemed smitten: like a kid gets smitten with a first love. I'm sorry, Ma, but I think you are going to have that kind of trouble with him now."

Ma's face tightened and her eyes snapped.

"You aren't kidding, are you?"

"No. When you see them together, you'll know I'm right. He seemed anxious for her to have the diamonds. He's got them. Have you forgotten?"

"I haven't forgotten," Ma said grimly. "He'll give them to me when I ask for them. So you really think he's fallen for this girl?"

"I'm sure of it."

"I'll soon stop that," Ma said. "I'm not having woman trouble in this house!"

"Don't be too sure," Doc said gravely. "Slim's dangerous. He could turn on you. The trouble with you, Ma, is you won't face up to the fact he isn't normal..."

"Shut up!" Ma snarled. This was a forbidden subject. "I'm not listening to that crap. Slim's all right I can handle him. Leave it that way."

Doc shrugged. He took a drink. His face was beginning to flush. It took very little liquor now to make Doc drunk.

"Don't say I didn't warn you."

"I want you to write a letter to Blandish," Ma said, changing the subject. "Well deliver it tomorrow. Tell him to have the money ready in a white suitcase. He is to put an ad in the Tribune, to appear the day after tomorrow, offering kegs of white paint for sale. That'll tell us the money is ready. Warn him what will happen to the girl if he tries a double cross."

"All right, Ma," Doc said and taking his glass, he left the room.

The old woman sat for some time, thinking. What Doc had told her, disturbed her. If Slim had fallen for this girl, then the sooner she was got rid of the better. She tried to convince herself Doc was exaggerating. Slim had always been scared of girls. She had watched him grow up. She was sure he had never had any sexual experience.

She got to her feet.

I'd better talk to him, she thought. I'll get the necklace from him. I'll have to be careful how I sell it. Maybe it would be safer to keep it for a while. It'll be hotter than a stove for months.

She went upstairs to Slim's room.

Slim was lying on his bed in his shirt and trousers. The necklace was dangling between his bony fingers. As Ma entered the room, the necklace disappeared with the same incredible speed with which he could produce his knife.

Quick as he was, Ma saw the necklace although she didn't say so.

"What are you lying down for?" she demanded, advancing up to the bed. "You tired or something?"

Slim scowled at her. There were times when his mother

bored him with her stupid questions.

"Yeah I'm tired. I didn't want to listen to all that talk downstairs."

"You should be thankful I can talk," Ma said grimly. "We're going to be rich, Slim. That girl's worth a pile of money to us."

Slim's face lit up and his scowl went away.

"Where is she, Ma?"

Ma stared at him. She had never seen such an expression on his face before. She stiffened, thinking, so Doc's right. The poor fool looks smitten. I wouldn't have believed it.

"She's in the front room under lock and key," she said.

Slim rolled over on his back, staring up at the ceiling.

"She's pretty, isn't she, Ma?" he said, simpering. "I've never seen any girl like her. Did you see her hair?"

"Pretty?" Ma snarled. "Why should you care? She's just like any other girl."

Slim turned his head and stared at her. He looked surprised.

"You think that?" he asked. "Haven't you eyes in your head? What's the matter with you? I've always thought you were smart. She's beautiful. If you can't see it, you must be blind." He ran his fingers through his greasy long hair. "She's like something out of a picture book. I want to keep her, Ma. We don't have to send her back, do we? We'll get the money and I'll keep her. I've never had a girl. She's going to be my girl."

"Yeah?" Ma sneered. "Do you think she'll want you? Look at your hands and shirt. They're filthy. Do you imagine a snooty little bitch like her will look at you?"

Slim examined his hands. He seemed suddenly unsure of himself.

"I guess I could wash," he said as if it was an idea that had never occurred to him before. "I could put on a clean shirt."

"I haven't time to waste talking this crap," Ma said roughly. "I want the necklace."

Slim eyed her, his head cocked on one side. Then he took the necklace from his pocket and dangled it out of Ma's reach. There was a sudden look of cunning on his face that Ma didn't like.

"It's pretty, isn't it?" he said. "But you're not having it. I'm keeping it. I know you—if you had it, you'd sell it. That's all you think about—money. I'm going to give it back to her. It's hers."

Ma controlled her rising temper.

"Hand that necklace to me!" she grated, holding out her hand.

Slim slid off the bed and faced her, his eyes gleaming.

"I'm keeping it."

This had never happened to Ma before. For a moment she was so surprised, she didn't know quite what to do, then her temper exploded and she advanced on Slim, swinging her great fists.

"Goddamn it! Give it to me before I hit you!" she shouted, her heavy face mottled and furious.

"Keep back!" Suddenly his knife jumped into his hand. He crouched, glaring at his mother. "Keep back!"

Ma came to an abrupt standstill. Looking at the thin, vicious face and the gleaming yellow eyes, she remembered Doc's warning. She felt a chill crawl up her spine.

"Put that knife away, Slim," she said quietly. "What do you think you're doing?"

Slim eyed her, then suddenly he grinned.

"That scared you, didn't it, Ma? I saw you were scared. You're like the rest of them. Even you are scared of me."

"Don't talk foolish," Ma said. "You're my son. Why should I be scared of you? Now come on, give me the necklace."

"I'll tell you what we'll do," Slim said, a crafty expression on his face. "You want the necklace: I want the girl. We'll trade. You fix it she likes me: I give you the diamonds. How's that?"

"Why, you poor fool..." Ma began but stopped when Slim dropped the necklace into his pocket.

"You're not having it until the girl's nice to me," he said. "You talk to her, Ma. Tell her I won't hurt her I want her to keep me company. Those punks downstairs don't like me. You've got Doc to talk to. I've got no one. I want her."

While he was talking, Ma was thinking. Even if she had the necklace, she couldn't get rid of it yet. It would be months before she would dare try to sell it. It wasn't important that he should keep it for a while. What was important was this show of rebellion and her loss of authority. She eyed the knife in her son's hand. She again remembered Doc's warning. It was true. Slim wasn't normal. He was dangerous. She wasn't going to risk getting a knife stuck in her. It would be better to do what he wanted. It wouldn't be for long. When the ransom was paid, the girl would go and Slim would forget about her and settle down. Maybe it might be a good idea for him to have a little fun with the girl. If he fancied this one, why not let him have her? Doc was always talking about frustrations and repressions. Yes, it might be an idea to let Slim have the girl. It might be good for him: give him something else to think about instead of staying in his room.

"Put that knife away, Slim," she said moving away from him. "I don't see any reason why you shouldn't amuse yourself with the girl. I'll see what I can do. Put it away. You should be ashamed to threaten your mother with a knife."

Slim suddenly realized he had won a victory. He giggled.

"Now you're talking sense," he said and put the knife away. "You fix it, Ma, and I'll give you the necklace, but you've got to fix it good."

"I'll talk to her," Ma said and went slowly from the room.

This was the first time Slim had ever got the better of her and she didn't like it.

Doc's right, she thought, as she plodded down the stairs. He's dangerous. He could get worse. The hell of it is, I'm getting old. Soon I won't be able to handle him at all.

2

As soon as Eddie got into town, he parked the Buick and then bought a newspaper.

The kidnapping of Miss Blandish and the murder of Jerry MacGowan were spread across the front page. He read the account quickly. There was nothing there new to him. The Chief of Police said he was following an important clue, but he didn't say what it was. Eddie guessed that was just bluff.

He walked to a cigar store at the corner of the street. He nodded to the fat man behind the counter and passed through a curtained doorway into the poolroom.

The room was thick with smoke and full of men, drinking and playing pool. Eddie looked around and spotted Woppy by himself keeping a bottle of Scotch company.

"Hi," Eddie said, coming over and sitting down. "What's

cooking?"

Woppy signaled to the barman to bring another glass.

"Plenty," Woppy said. "Have you seen the papers?"

"Nothing in them," Eddie said. He nodded to the barman as he set the glass on the table. He poured himself a drink.

"You wait for the evening edition. Remember the punk who collects dirt for Gossip? Heinie? He's shot his mouth off to the cops."

"What's the idea? Since when has he been an informer?"

"The insurance people are offering a reward for the necklace. I guess Heinie wants the dough. He's told the cops Bailey was interested in the necklace. They've turned over the town but they can't find Bailey so they're saying he and Riley pulled the snatch. Good for us, huh?"

Eddie grinned.

"I'll say."

"The Feds have taken over. They've seen Blandish. The town's lousy with cops. You'd better watch out they don't catch you with your rod."

"I left it at home. I'm phoning Blandish right now and then I'm blowing. You'd better come with me."

"Okay." As Eddie got to his feet, Woppy asked, "How's the redhead? Boy! Wouldn't I like to get close to that one!"

"Better not," Eddie said. "Ma's on the warpath. She says to lay off the girl: got quite steamed up about it."

Woppy pulled a face.

"There are times when Ma gives me a pain. What's the good of having a doll like that in the house if you can't make use of her?"

"The answer to that one is a million bucks," Eddie said, grinning. He crossed over to the telephone booth but from the sign on the door, it was out of order. There was a booth in a drugstore across the way. He left the cigar store and paused on the edge of the curb for a gap in the traffic. While he waited, he noticed a girl standing by a nearby bus stop. She immediately attracted his attention: every good-looking girl did. She was a tall, cool-looking blonde with a figure that made him look twice. She had a pert prettiness that appealed to Eddie. He studied her face for a brief moment. Her make-up was good. Her mouth was a trifle large, but Eddie didn't mind that. He liked the sexy look she had and the sophisticated way she wore her yellow summery dress.

Some dish, he thought I wouldn't mind being shipwrecked with her.

He crossed the road and entered the drugstore. He shut himself in the telephone booth. Then hanging a handkerchief over the mouthpiece of the telephone to muffle the sound of his voice, he dialed the number he had got from Miss Blandish and waited.

He didn't have to wait long. A voice said, "Hello? This is John Blandish talking. Who is it, please?"

"Listen carefully, pal," Eddie said, making his voice hard and tough. "We've got your daughter. If you want her back, call off the cops. We want a million dollars for her. Get the money together in used bills, no bill larger than a hundred and put the money in a white suitcase. You'll get delivery instructions tomorrow. Got all that?"

"Yes." Blandish's voice was strained and anxious. "Is she all right?"

"She's fine and she'll remain fine just so long as you do what you're told. If you try anything smart she's in for a bad time and when I say bad, I mean bad. I don't have to draw you a blue-print. You can imagine what'll happen to her before we rub her out. It's up to you, pal. She'll be okay just as long as you do what we tell you. If you don't, you'll get her back very soiled—and very dead!" He slammed down the receiver arid walked quickly out of the drugstore, grinning to himself.

Across the road, as he again waited for a gap in the traffic, he saw the blonde girl still waiting at the bus stop. She glanced at him and then away. Eddie fingered his tie. He thought it was too bad he had to report back to Ma. He crossed the road and again looked at the girl, ready to smile at her, but she wasn't looking at him. He moved to the cigar store and paused to look back. The girl was coming towards him. He stood waiting. She didn't look at him. As she passed close to him, a white card fluttered out of her hand and fell at his feet. She neither paused nor looked at him. He stared after her, watching the sensuous movement of her hips, then he picked up the card. On it was scribbled: 243, *Palace Hotel, West.*

He pushed his hat to the back of his head, surprised. He

hadn't taken the girl for a hooker. He was vaguely disappointed. He looked after her and was in time to see her get into a taxi. He watched the taxi drive away, then he slipped the card under the strap of his wrist watch. Maybe when he had a little more time, he thought, entering the cigar store, he'd call on her.

"All fixed," he said to Woppy. "Let's get out of here."

Woppy finished his drink, paid the barman and the two men walked down the street to where Eddie had parked the Buick. A Ford had just pulled into a parking space across the road. Two powerfully built men were in the car. Both of them were staring at Eddie and Woppy.

"Feds," Woppy said without moving his lips.

Eddie unlocked the Buick. He could feel cold sweat on his face. They got into the car. Both of them took tremendous care to seem casual. The two men in the Ford still watched them. Eddie started the car and drove into the stream of traffic.

"Don't look back," he warned Woppy.

After a few minutes, they relaxed.

"Those punks give me the shakes," Eddie said. "The less I have to do with them, the better my blood pressure."

"You can say that again," Woppy said with feeling. "This town's crawling with them."

They arrived back as Flynn was getting out of a battered Dodge. The three men went into Ma's room.

"Okay?" she asked Flynn.

"Yeah. No trouble at all," he said. "No one was around. I didn't even have to get out of the car. He came out to fill my tank; when he had filled it, I let him have it. Nothing to it."

Ma nodded. She looked at Eddie.

"I told him," Eddie said. "I didn't give him a chance to talk back, but he knows what to expect if he starts anything smart. The town's full of Feds, Ma. The heat's on good." He tossed the newspaper onto the table. "Nothing in that we don't already know. Heinie's been to the cops. He's told them Bailey was asking questions about the necklace. The cops are hunting for him and Riley."

"I reckoned that would happen," Ma said with her wolfish grin. "So long as they don't dig up those stiffs, we'll be in the clear. This is working out right."

"When the girl's returned," Eddie said seriously, "we'll be in trouble. She'll talk."

Ma stared at him.

"What makes you think she's going to be returned?"

"Yeah." Eddie shook his head. He glanced at Woppy who grimaced. "Seems a hell of a waste of a woman."

"To hell with her!" Flynn broke in savagely. "We've got to think of ourselves."

"Who's going to do it?" Eddie said. "Not me!"

"Nor me," Woppy said.

"Doc will give her a shot in the arm when she's asleep," Ma said. "If he won't, I will."

"When?" Flynn asked.

"When I'm good and ready," Ma snapped. "You leave me to worry about that."

Eddie sat down and poured himself a drink.

"Say, Ma, let's have another look at the necklace. I didn't get a chance to look at it properly."

"It's in the safe," Ma lied. "Some other time." To change the subject, she asked, "Why don't one of you lazy slobs get dinner ready?"

Woppy got to his feet.

"Oh, hell! Spaghetti again!" Eddie groaned. "Hey, Flynn, can't you cook?"

Flynn grinned.

"As good as you," he said.

Eddie lifted his shoulders in despair.

"What we want around here is a woman."

"And that's what you're not going to have," Ma said coldly, "Get going, Woppy. I want my dinner."

Eddie had taken the card he had picked up from under his watch strap. He read the address again. He thought of the girl. He decided he'd call on her that night. He turned the card and noticed for the first time there was a message written on it.

He read the message, then with a startled curse, he jumped to his feet. Written in a feminine hand were the words: What have you done with Frankie Riley?

3

As a street clock was striking eleven, the Buick slid to a

standstill near the Palace Hotel. Eddie and Flynn got out, leaving Woppy at the wheel.

"Stick around," Eddie said. "If you see any cops, move off, but keep circling. We may need you in a hurry."

"Rather you than me," Woppy said and stuck a cigarette on his lip.

Eddie and Flynn walked quickly down the street to the hotel entrance. It wasn't much of a place. They walked into the lobby which was empty. Behind the desk dozed a fat, elderly man in his shirt sleeves. He blinked open his eyes as Eddie came up.

"You want a room?" the man asked hopefully, getting to his feet.

"No. Who's in 243?" Eddie asked curtly.

The man stiffened.

"Can't give you information like that," he said.

"You'd better call around tomorrow morning and ask at the desk."

Flynn took out his gun and shoved it into the man's face.

"You heard what the guy said, didn't you?" he snarled.

The man's face went white at the sight of the gun. With trembling hands, he thumbed through the register. Eddie snatched it from him. He ran his finger quickly down the list of numbers.

"Anna Borg," he said when he arrived at No 243. "Who's she?" He noted the rooms either side of 243 were vacant.

Flynn slid the gun in his hand and held it by the barrel. He reached forward and clubbed the man on top of his head. The man slid down behind the counter. Eddie craned his neck to look at him.

"You shouldn't have hit him that hard," he said. "He looks like a family man. Better tie him up."

Flynn went around and tied the man's hands behind him with the man's tie. Leaving him behind the counter, they walked over to the elevator and rode up to the second floor.

"You stay here," Eddie said, "and watch the stairs. I'll call on the dame."

He started off down the passage, looking for room 243.

He found it at the far end of the passage. He listened, his ear against the door panel. Then he drew his gun and stepped into the dark room. He shut the door, groped for the light switch and turned it on.

He looked around. The small room was empty and untidy. Clothes were scattered on the bed and chair. He recognized the yellow dress the girl had been wearing hanging over the chair back. The dressing table was crowded with cosmetic bottles. The contents of a large powder box had been tipped onto the carpet. When he was satisfied no one was in the room and there was nowhere for anyone to hide, he opened drawers but found nothing to interest him. He wondered where the girl had got to. He left the room, shutting the door and joined Flynn at the head of the stairs. "She isn't around."

"Let's get out of here," Flynn said. "The room next to hers is empty," Eddie said. "We'll wait in there. She may come back."

"How about the guy downstairs? What happens if someone finds him?"

"I'll worry about that when he's found," Eddie said. "Come on."

They went silently down the passage to room 241, opened the door and entered. Eddie left the door open a couple of inches. He stood by the door while Flynn went and lay on the bed.

Minutes dragged by. Then just when he was beginning to think he was wasting his time, Eddie heard a sound that alerted him and brought Flynn off the bed and to the door. Both men peered through the crack in the door.

The door exactly opposite room 243 was opening slowly. A girl appeared and looked up and down the passage. Eddie recognized her immediately: she was the blonde he had seen in the street. Before he could make up his mind what to do, she had come out, shut the door and then had run across the passage and into room 243. They heard the door shut and the key turn.

"That the dame?" Flynn asked, breathing hard down Eddie's neck. "Yeah."

"Nice," Flynn said. "What's she been up to?"

Eddie opened the door wide and moved into the passage.

"I don't know, but I'm going to find out. You go to the stairs."

Flynn went off down the passage.

Eddie crossed to the opposite door. He turned the handle

and pressed. The door opened. He looked into darkness. He listened, heard nothing. He entered the room.

He turned on the light switch, then he caught his breath sharply. A short fat man lay on the floor. Blood was running from a wound in his head. He had been shot. Eddie didn't have to go closer to see the man was dead.

4

Ma Grisson had been brooding for some time. There was an expression on her face that warned Doc Williams not to bother her. Doc was playing solitaire. He kept looking at Ma, wondering what was going on in her mind. After a while her stillness got on his nerves and he put down his cards.

"Is there anything worrying you, Ma?" he asked cautiously.

"You get on with your game and leave me alone," Ma growled.

Doc lifted his shoulders. He got up and went to the front door, opened it and looked into the moonlit darkness. Lighting a cigar, he sat on the top step.

Ma suddenly got to her feet as if she had finally made up her mind. She went over to a cupboard and took from it a length of rubber hose.

Doc heard her movements and he looked around. He saw her climbing the stairs and he saw the rubber hose in her hand. He wondered vaguely what she was doing with it.

Ma Grisson went along the passage to the front room. She unlocked the door and entered the room. It was a small room. The window was covered with planks. There was only a chair, a small table and a mirror on the wall in the room. The threadbare carpet was dirty.

Ma shut the door and looked at Miss Blandish who was sitting up in bed, her eyes wide with alarm. In place of a nightgown she was wearing her slip. Ma sat on the bed. The springs sagged under her great weight.

"I've something to say to you," she said. "Have you ever been hit with a thing like this?" She held up the rubber hose.

Miss Blandish shook her head. She had just woken up out of a troubled sleep. This visit seemed a continuation of her nightmare.

"It hurts," the old woman said. She hit Miss Blandish on her knee. Although the blanket absorbed some of the blow, it stung. Miss Blandish stiffened. The sleepy look went out of her eyes. She struggled up in bed, clenching her fists; her eyes flashing angrily.

"Don't you dare touch me again!" she said breathlessly.

Ma Grisson grinned. Her big white teeth made her look wolfish and strangely like her son.

"So what would you do?"

She grabbed Miss Blandish's wrists in one of her huge hands. She sat grinning as the girl wrenched and pulled in a useless attempt to get free.

"Don't kid yourself," Ma said. "I may be old, but I'm much stronger than you. Now I'm going to take some of the starch out of you. Then we'll have a talk."

Downstairs, Doc, still sitting on the step, saw Woppy get out of the Buick and come towards him.

"Eddie back yet?" Woppy asked.

"No. What's happened?"

Woppy pushed past Doc and went into the sitting room. Doc followed him. Woppy picked up a bottle, held it up to the light, then threw it across the room in disgust.

"Isn't there ever anything to drink in this joint?"

Doc went to the cupboard and opened a new bottle of Scotch.

"What's happened to Eddie?" he asked as he made two stiff drinks.

"I don't know," Woppy said, taking one of the drinks. "We went to the hotel and he and Flynn went in. I hung around, then I saw a couple of cops. I moved off, circled the block and when I got back, I heard shooting. More cops started arriving so I beat it."

"Sounds as if Eddie's walked into trouble."

Woppy shrugged. He emptied his glass.

"He can take care of himself. I should worry." He paused and cocked his head on one side. "What's that?"

Doc stiffened and looked uneasily up at the ceiling.

"Sounds like the girl screaming."

"I'll go up and see," Woppy said, starting for the door.

"Better not," Doc said. "Ma's with her."

The two men listened to the high-pitched screaming for a moment, then Woppy, grimacing, went over to the radio and turned it on. The sudden blast of jazz drowned out the screams.

"Maybe I'm getting soft," Woppy said, wiping his face with his handkerchief, "but there are times when that bitch makes me sick to my stomach."

Doc drained his glass, then refilled it.

"Better not let her hear you say so," he said and sat down.

Upstairs Ma Grisson was once more sitting on the bed, breathing hard through her thick nose. She watched Miss Blandish writhing on the bed, tears running down her face, her hands twisting the sheet.

"Now I think we can talk," Ma said.

She began to speak. What she said made the girl forget her pain. She stared at the old woman as if she couldn't believe she was hearing correctly. Suddenly she gasped, "No!" Ma went on talking. Miss Blandish sat up and recoiled to the head of the bed, saying "No!"

At last Ma lost patience.

"You can't get out of it, you little fool!" she snarled. "You're going to do what I tell you! If you don't, I'll beat you again."

"No... No... No!"

Ma got to her feet and picked up the length of rubber hose. Then she changed her mind.

"I'm spoiling your pretty skin," she said, "and that won't do. There are other ways. I'll get Doc to fix you. I should have thought of that before. Yeah, Doc'll know how to fix you."

She went out of the room leaving Miss Blandish, her head buried in the pillow, sobbing wildly:

5

Eddie stared down at Heinie's body, feeling sweat break out on his face. If the cops walked in now he would be in a hell of a jam, he was thinking. He looked quickly around the room. There had been no struggle. He guessed someone had knocked on the door and when Heinie had opened it, he had been shot. From the small wound in Heinie's head, Eddie surmised the gun used had been a .25—a woman's weapon.

He touched Heinie's hand. It was still warm. Heinie hadn't

been dead longer than half an hour, if that.

Eddie looked into the passage. Flynn was still watching the stairs. Eddie left the room. As an afterthought he carefully wiped the door knob with his handkerchief. Then he crossed to room 243 and tried the door handle. The door was locked. He knocked. Flynn looked down the passage at him. Eddie rapped on the door again. There was no answer. He put his ear against the door panel. He heard the sound of the window being pushed open.

"Hey, you in there," he called softly. "Come on! Open up!"

Then the silence of the night was split by a woman's wild screams. From the sound, the woman in 243 was leaning out of the window, yelling her head off.

Eddie jumped back from the door.

"Come on, stupid!" Flynn shouted. "Let's get out of here!"

Eddie joined him at the head of the stairs and together the two men started down.

"Wait!" Flynn hissed and grabbed Eddie's arm. He looked down the well of the staircase into the hall. Eddie peered over Flynn's shoulder. Two cops, guns in hand, were standing in the hall. Suddenly, they moved to the stairs and started up them.

Eddie and Flynn spun around and darted up to the next landing. They could hear people shouting and doors opening.

"The roof!" Eddie panted.

They rushed up to the top landing. They could hear the cops pounding up after them. As they started down the long passage a door nearby opened and a scared-looking man poked his head out. Flynn hit him as he crowded past. The man fell down. From inside the room, a woman started to scream.

There was a door at the end of the passage which led out onto the roof. It was locked. Flynn fired two shots at the lock, then kicked the door open. The noise of the shots in the confined space deafened the two men. Gasping for breath, they stumbled out onto the flat roof and into the cool night air.

Running to the edge of the roof, they took a stiff drop onto the roof of the adjacent building, some fifteen feet below. The moon, hidden behind a cloud, made just enough light for them to see where they were going.

They paused for a moment, trying to decide which way they should go.

"We'd better split up," Eddie said. "You go left, I'll go right. Be seeing you."

Flynn moved off across the roof away from Eddie. There was a sudden shout and Flynn turned in time to see shadowy figures appearing on the upper roof. He fired. One of the figures dropped, and he darted into the darkness.

Screened by a row of chimney stacks, Eddie paused to look down into the street. People were coming out of the various apartment blocks and crowding the streets. A police car was pulling up. From it spilled four cops. They shoved their way through the crowd to the entrance of the hotel. In the distance came the sound of approaching sirens.

Eddie moved off. He lowered himself onto another roof. Crouching in the shadows, he looked back. The roof of the hotel was now alive with moving shadows. A gun banged away from him. One of the shadows slumped out of sight.

Eddie stood, hesitating. None of the cops seemed to be coming his way. They were chasing Flynn. Eddie grinned uneasily. It had been a smart idea to split up.

He moved across the roof to a skylight. His best bet, he told himself, was to get into the building and hide up until it was safe to leave.

Suddenly, without warning, a cop came from behind a chimney stack. The two men gaped at each other, for a moment paralyzed with shock and surprise, then the cop acted quickly. He jerked up his gun, but Eddie was a shade faster. He slammed a punch at the cop's head and brought his gun butt down on the cop's gun wrist. The cop reeled back, dropping his gun. Eddie could have shot him, but he knew the sound of the shooting would bring the other cops.

He jumped forward, took a stiff blow to the side of his face from the cop and clubbed the cop with his gun butt.

The cop was tough and full of fight. He was trying to pull his nightstick. He and Eddie grappled. For a long moment, the two men strained together, then Eddie punched the cop off. As he came forward again, Eddie sidestepped him and hit him a crushing blow with the gun butt on the side of his head. The cop dropped like a pole-axed bull.

Panting, Eddie looked anxiously around. He could hear distant shooting. He ran over to the skylight and jerked it open.

The bolt holding it in place was flimsy and it snapped at his first heave. He looked into the darkness, then swung his legs into space and dropped. He took out his flashlight and sent the beam around the room. It was full of boxes, trunks and unwanted furniture. Moving to the door, he opened it cautiously and peered out into a dark passage. He listened, then moving forward, he reached the head of the stairs. He turned off his flashlight and made his way down to the lower landing.

Police sirens were now making a deafening noise. He could hear the sound of running footsteps. There was a great deal of distant shouting. He reached the landing and peered over the banisters. Far below, he saw three cops starting up the stairs towards him.

Sweat was running down his face now. This was getting much too hot for comfort, he was thinking.

He whipped around and noiselessly entered the first room near him. The light was on in the room. A woman was leaning far out of the window, looking down at the commotion going on in the street below. He could only see her pyjamaed back and legs, and even under this pressure, he found himself thinking she had a nice shape.

He closed the door and tiptoed across to the woman. He stood close to her, waiting. She must have sensed she was no longer alone for she suddenly straightened and whirled around.

Eddie pounced on her; one hand clamped over her mouth, the other gripped her wrists.

"Make a sound and I'll break your neck!" he said, holding her against him.

She stared up at him. She was only a kid: she couldn't have been more than eighteen. Her blue eyes opened very wide. She looked so scared he thought she was going to faint.

"Take it easy," he said. "I'm not going to hurt you if you don't make a noise."

She leaned heavily against him, closing her eyes. He could hear the sound of voices and tramping of feet coming along the passage.

He gave the girl a little shake.

"The cops are looking for me," he said. "You'll be all right if you don't make a noise and do what I tell you. Come on, get into bed."

He carried her over to the bed and slid her under the sheet.

"Don't make a sound," he warned as he took his hand from her mouth.

"I—I won't," she said breathlessly, staring up at him.

"Good girl."

He turned off the light, plunging the room into darkness. He lay down on the floor by the side of the bed away from the door.

"If they come in here and find me," he said, drawing his gun, "there's going to be shooting and you could get damaged. So don't start yelling."

"I won't," the girl said, more confidence in her voice now.

He could hear doors opening and people talking excitedly. It sounded as if the cops were going from room to room.

"It's up to you, baby," he said from the floor, "to stall them if they come in here." He slid his hand under the sheet and took her hand in his. He was surprised she squeezed his hand and he winked to himself in the darkness. "You don't have to be scared of me."

"I'm not scared," she said.

They waited. He could hear her fast breathing and his own heart beats.

Suddenly heavy footfalls sounded outside. The door opened cautiously. Eddie lifted his gun. The girl gripped his hand hard. The beam of a powerful flashlight swung around the room. The girl gave a little scream. "Who is it?" she quavered. The light fell on her.

"Police," a voice growled from behind the light. "You alone in here?"

"Yes... what is it?"

"A couple of gunmen loose," the cop said. "Nothing for you to worry about. You should lock your door, miss."

The door closed and the heavy footsteps receded.

Eddie drew in a deep breath. He let go of the girl's hand, got to his feet and went over to the door and turned the key in the lock. He came back to the bed and sat on the floor.

"Thanks, baby," he said. "You did a nice job. I'll stay here until it's quiet, then I'll beat it. Relax, you don't have to worry about me."

The girl didn't say anything. She stared curiously at him, just able to make him out in the dim light coming through the uncurtained window.

After some minutes, Eddie found the floor getting hard. He got up and sat on the end of the bed.

"I'm getting calluses," he said, grinning. "You get off to sleep if you want to."

"I don't want to sleep," the girl said. "You scared the life out of me, but I'm not so scared now."

"That's fine," Eddie said. "I scared the life out of myself too."

The sounds in the building had died down. Some of the police cars were moving off. He wondered if Flynn had got away. He guessed he had. Flynn knew how to take care of himself.

After a long pause, the girl said, "It was just like a movie. All that shooting... if you hadn't held my hand I would have screamed."

Eddie looked at her with growing interest.

"I'll hold it again any time you like."

She gave a nervous giggle.

"I don't feel like screaming now."

He got up and looked out of the window. The crowded street was now deserted. The last of the police cars were moving away.

"Well, I guess I can go. Looks like the show is over." He came over to the bed and smiled at the girl. "Thanks a lot, baby. You were swell."

She half sat up in the bed.

"Are you sure it's safe to go?"

"Yeah. I can't stay here all night."

She settled down in the bed.

"Can't you?" She spoke so softly he scarcely heard what she said, but he did hear. He suddenly grinned.

"Well, there's no law against it, is there? Do you want me to stay?"

"Now you're making me blush," the girl said and hid her face. "What a question to ask a lady."

6

Two days later, an advertisement offering kegs of white paint appeared in the *Tribune*.

Ma Grisson tossed the newspaper to Doc.

"The money's ready," she said. "Now we've got to collect it.

It'll be a soft job, Flynn and Woppy can handle it. You write to Blandish, Doc. Tell him to drive to the Maxwell filling station on Highway 71. He'll know where it is. He's to get to the Blue Hills golf course at one o'clock." She looked over at Flynn and Woppy who were listening. "That's where you boys will be waiting. He is to throw the suitcase out of the car window when he sees a light flashing. He's not to stop. Warn him he'll be watched from the moment he leaves his house. If he cooperates with the police or tries anything smart, the girl will suffer." To Flynn and Woppy, she went on, "You won't have any trouble. Blandish will be too scared something might happen to the girl. The road's straight for miles. If you're followed, drop the suitcase in the road so they can see it, and keep moving. They won't come after you because of the girl."

"Tomorrow night?" Flynn asked.

"That's it."

Flynn stuck a cigarette on his lower lip.

"Didn't you say the girl was to be knocked off, Ma?" he said, staring at Ma. "What are we keeping her for?"

Ma stiffened. Her little eyes turned hard.

"She'll go when we get the money."

"Why wait?"

"Who do you think you're talking to?" Ma snarled. "Shut your loose mouth!"

Flynn looked over at Doc who couldn't meet his direct stare. Doc got up, muttered something under his breath and left the room.

"What's happening to the girl, Ma?" Flynn asked. "I saw that old quack go into her room last night with a hypo."

Ma's face turned purple.

"Did you? If you've nothing better to do than to snoop around here, I'll have to find you something to do."

The tone of her voice alarmed Flynn.

"Okay, okay," he said hastily. "I was only shooting the breeze."

"Shoot it to someone who wants to listen," Ma snarled. "Get out of here!"

Flynn hurriedly left the room. After a moment's uneasy hesitation, Woppy followed him. The two men went upstairs and into Eddie's room.

Eddie was in bed, reading the Sunday comics.

"Hi, you misbegotten freaks!" he said cheerfully. "What's cooking?"

Flynn sat on the foot of the bed. Woppy straddled a chair, laying his fat arms along the back.

"We're collecting the dough tomorrow night," Woppy said. "The ad's in the *Tribune*."

"A million bucks!" Eddie said, lying back on the dirty pillow. "Think of it! At last, we're in the money!"

"What are you going to do with your cut when you get it?" Woppy asked.

"I'm going to buy an island in the South Seas," Eddie said, "and I'm going to stock it with beautiful girls in grass skirts."

Woppy laughed, slapping his fat thigh.

"You and your women! Me—I'm going to start a restaurant. My spaghetti's going to be world famous."

Flynn, who had been listening, his vicious face disinterested, suddenly asked, "What's going on in the girl's room, Eddie?"

Eddie stopped laughing and stared at Flynn.

"What do you mean?"

"What I say. I'm in the room next to hers and I hear things. Doc goes in there. I've seen him with a hypo. Slim sneaks in there too. He was in there from eleven last night to four in the morning."

Eddie threw the sheet off and got out of bed. "What do you mean—a hypo?"

"You heard me. Doc had a hypo in his hand when he went into her room. Do you think he's drugging her?"

"Why should he?"

"I don't know—I'm asking you. Why does Slim go in there?" Eddie started to throw on his clothes.

"Slim! You don't think that poisonous moron has ideas about the girl, do you?"

"I tell you I don't know, but Ma's goddamn touchy when I mention the girl."

"I'm going to talk to her," Eddie said. "I'm not standing for Slim relieving his repressions on that girl. There's a limit, and goddamn it, that would be the limit!"

"You'd better not," Woppy said in alarm. "Ma won't like it.

Better keep out of it."

Eddie ignored him; to Flynn he said, "Watch the stairs. Give me a tip if it looks like Ma's coming up."

"Sure," Flynn said and went out into the passage. He leaned over the banister.

Eddie ran a comb through his hair, put on a tie, then went quickly down the passage to Miss Blandish's room. The key was in the lock. He turned it and entered the room.

Miss Blandish lay flat on her back on the bed, covered by a grimy sheet. She was staring up at the ceiling.

Eddie closed the door and went over to her.

"Hello, baby," he said. "How are you getting on?"

Miss Blandish didn't seem to know he was in the room. She continued to stare up at the ceiling.

Eddie put his hand on her shoulder and shook her gently.

"Wake up, baby," he said. "What's going on?"

Slowly, she turned her head and stared at him. Her eyes were blank: the pupils enormously enlarged.

"Go away," she said, her words blurred.

He sat on the bed.

"You know me—I'm Eddie," he said. "Wake up! What's going on?"

She closed her eyes. For several minutes he watched her, then suddenly she began to speak. Her low, lifeless voice was like a medium in a trance talking.

"I wish I was dead," she said. "They say nothing matters once you are dead." There was another long pause, while Eddie frowned down at her, then she went on. "Dreams... nothing but horrible dreams. There's a man who comes here, who seems very real, but he doesn't really exist. He is tall and thin and he smells of dirt. He stands over me and talks. I don't understand what he is saying." She moved under the sheet as if its weight was unbearable to her. There was again a long pause of silence, then she went on, "I pretend to be dead. I want to scream when he comes in, but if I did, he would know I was alive. He stands for hours by me, mumbling." Then suddenly she screamed out, *"Why doesn't he do something to me?"*

Eddie started back, sweat on his face. The awful tone of her scream frightened him. He looked towards the door, wondering if Ma had heard her.

Miss Blandish relaxed again. She was muttering now, moving her body uneasily, her hands twisting the sheet.

"I wish he would do something to me," she said. "Anything is better than having him standing hour after hour at my side, talking. I wish he would do something to me..."

Flynn poked his head around the door.

"You'd better get out of here. What's she yelling about?"

Eddie shoved him out of the room and shut and locked the door. He wiped his sweating face with the back of his hand.

"What's going on in there?" Flynn demanded.

"Something pretty bad," Eddie said. "She'd be better off dead."

"Nobody's better off dead," Flynn said sharply. "What do you mean?"

Eddie went back to his room. Flynn trailed along behind him.

As Eddie entered, Woppy looked up at him, startled by his bleak expression.

"Get out of here!" Eddie snarled and went over to his bed and lay down on it.

Woppy went quickly out of the room. He looked blankly at Flynn who shrugged his shoulders.

Eddie shut his eyes. For the first time in his life he felt dirty and ashamed of himself.

7

POLICE SUSPECT RILEY GANG RESPONSIBLE FOR POLICE SLAYING
Murdered man identified.
John Blandish pays ransom money.

Our reporter learns the man shot to death at the Palace Hotel has been identified as Alvin Heinie, the free-lance society gossip writer. It was Heinie who informed the police that the Riley mob had questioned him concerning the movements of John Blandish's daughter, the kidnapped heiress.

It is understood that the ransom demand of a million dollars is being paid today. Mr. Blandish, fearing for his daughter's safety has refused to cooperate with the authorities. The Department of Justice and the Federal Bureau of

Investigation are standing by. They will go into immediate action when it is known the kidnapped girl is safe.

The police have reason to believe that Alvin Heinie was murdered by the Riley gang as an act of revenge...

Ma Grisson read the story to the gang who listened, grinning.

"Nice work," Flynn said. "Riley's getting blamed for everything. I bet if the Chief of Police fell downstairs, he would say Riley had pushed him." Eddie was looking thoughtful.

"Maybe it's okay, but I've been asking myself who did shoot Heinie. It wasn't Riley and it wasn't us. This Borg girl bothers me. I think she knocked Heinie off. Why? We do know she's connected in some way with Riley. I think we should do something about her."

"You're right," Ma said. "Before we collect the money, we must find out where she fits in. You go into town, Eddie and ask around. You might get a lead on her."

"Okay," Eddie said getting to his feet. "You coming with me, Slim?"

Slim was sitting in a corner away from the rest of the mob. He was reading the comics. He didn't even look up when Eddie spoke to him.

"You go in alone," Ma said. "Leave your rod here." Eddie went out into the hall. Ma followed him. "You go and talk to Pete Cosmos," Ma said. "He knows all the girls in town. Gimme your gun."

As Eddie handed the .45 over, he said, "Can't you tell Slim to leave the girl alone, Ma?" Ma stiffened.

"Mind your own business, Eddie," she said. "You're a good boy. Don't start poking your nose into something that doesn't concern you."

"Come on, Ma," Eddie said coaxingly. "That girl's too nice to have Slim messing her around. Give her a break, can't you?"

Ma's eyes suddenly snapped with rage. Her face turned purple.

"Slim wants her," she said, lowering her voice and glaring at Eddie. "He's going to have her. You keep out of it! That goes for the rest of you too!"

Eddie showed his disgust.

"To hell with a punk who can only get a girl by filling her

with drugs," he said.

Ma struck him across the mouth with the back of her hand. It was a heavy blow and sent him back on his heels. They stared at each other, then Eddie forced a grin.

"Okay, Ma," he said. "I was talking out of turn. Forget it"

He left her glaring after him, her face dark with rage.

As he drove downtown, he told himself, he would have to be careful. Ma was as dangerous as Slim. She wouldn't hesitate to shoot him in the back if she thought he was going to cause trouble in the gang about the Blandish girl. He shrugged his shoulders. He felt sorry for the girl, but he wasn't going to risk his life for her.

He arrived at the Cosmos Club a little after two p.m. The cleaners were still clearing up after the night before. The girls were rehearsing under the direction of a little man, dressed in a blazer and white trousers. The pianist was pounding out jazz, a cigarette dangling from his lips. The girls, wearing shorts, all smiled at Eddie. He was well known at the club and popular. He paused long enough to pat a few sleek behinds and crack a joke before going on to the office.

Pete Cosmos was sitting at his desk, reading the newspaper. He seemed surprised when Eddie walked in. Pete was a fat ball of a man with a pencil-line moustache and a liking for violent, hand-painted ties. The tie he had on made Eddie blink.

They shook hands.

"Hi, Pete," Eddie said, sitting on the corner of the desk. "What's cooking?"

Pete tossed the newspaper on the floor. He shook his head, scowling.

"That's the trouble," he said, offering Eddie a cigar. "Nothing's cooking. Since all this shooting, business has gone to hell. We only had ten people in last night: four of them were my wife's friends and didn't pay."

"Yeah," Eddie said sympathetically. "I get the same story wherever I go. This punk Riley really seems to have started something."

Pete lit his cigar.

"I can't understand it, Eddie. I would never have believed Riley had the nerve to snatch that dame. He was strictly small time. He must have gone nuts. Now if it had been Ma who had pulled the job..."

"She didn't," Eddie said. "We've been out of town all week."

"Sure, sure," Pete said quickly catching the sudden hard note in Eddie's voice. "I haven't seen you or the boys for weeks. All the same, if I had snatched the girl, I'd be Very, very careful. As soon as the ransom's paid and the girl returned, the heat's going to be turned on that'll paralyze this town. You mark my words."

"It's Riley's funeral," Eddie said.

"I'd like to know where he's hiding," Pete said.

"Who's Anna Borg?" Eddie asked casually, studying the glowing tip of his cigar.

"What's she to you?" Pete asked sharply.

"I want to know who she is," Eddie said. "Do you know her?"

"Sure."

"Who is she? What does she do for a living?"

"She totes the gun," Pete said.

Eddie was surprised.

"Is that a fact? Who does she carry the gun for?"

Pete smiled.

"Who do you think? Riley."

Eddie whistled.

"Well, well! Certainly news to me."

"I'll tell you something else," Pete said. "Anna's been left high and dry and the boys are asking why. She and Riley were like that." He held up two dirty fingers close together. "Then Riley pulls the biggest snatch of the century and Anna's left out in the cold. It doesn't make sense."

"Maybe Riley got tired of her," Eddie said.

"The boys say not. Anna swears Riley wouldn't have ditched her. She thinks something's happened to him."

Eddie's face became expressionless.

"You know women," he said with a sneer. "They'd say anything to save their face. You can bet Riley's ditched her now he's heading for the big money. She just won't admit it."

Pete shrugged.

"Could be. Anyway, it's not my business."

"Is she still living at the Palace Hotel?"

Pete looked curiously at him.

"Why the interest in Anna?"

"Ma wants to know."

Pete looked surprised.

"Yeah, Anna's still at the Palace. She has a couple of dicks parked with her. The Feds think Riley came to see her, ran into Heinie who was staying there and couldn't resist knocking Heinie off for ratting on him. They think Riley might come back to see Anna so they're waiting for him."

Eddie rubbed his jaw, his mind busy. Finally, he said, "I want to talk to this baby, Pete. Here's what you do: telephone her right now and tell her to come here. I'll talk to her here and the Feds won't know we've met."

"What do you want to talk to her about?" Pete asked suspiciously. "I'm not getting Anna in trouble. She's okay with me."

"No trouble, Pete. Do what I say. Ma's orders."

Pete was scared of Ma. He called Anna's apartment.

"That you, Anna?" he asked while Eddie watched him. "This is Pete. Something's come up important. I want you over here right away. No, I don't say it's a job, but it might lead to one. You'll come? Okay, I'm waiting for you," and he hung up.

"Okay?" Eddie asked.

"She's coming. She'll be here in half an hour."

"Thanks, Pete. I'll tell Ma. She won't forget you."

"I'd rather she did forget me," Pete said uneasily. "And listen, Eddie, no rough stuff with Anna."

"Relax. I just want a brotherly talk with her." Eddie grinned. "Suppose you take a walk and leave me here. Come back in an hour."

Pete shrugged his shoulders.

"Well, it's time I had lunch. I guess I'd better have it."

"And Pete," Eddie said. "You got a gun?"

"What do you want a gun for?" Pete asked startled.

"Come on, come on! Don't talk so much. Have you got a gun?"

"In the top left hand drawer," Pete said.

"Okay. You take off."

When Pete had gone, Eddie went around and sat behind the desk. He opened the drawer and took out a .38 which he laid on the desk. He didn't intend to take any chances with a girl who carried a gun for Riley. Gun-girls had lots of nerve, and besides, he was pretty sure Anna had knocked Heinie off.

After a wait of thirty minutes, he heard the click of high heels coming down the passage. He put his hand on the gun.

The door swung open and Anna walked in. She was wearing a pale green summer dress and a big straw hat. Eddie thought she looked terrific.

She was halfway across the room before she saw him. She had swung the door to as she had entered. She stopped short, the color leaving her face. Her eyes went to the gun on the desk.

"Hello, baby," Eddie said. "Come on in. Keep your pants on. This is a friendly meeting, but let's have your handbag. Pass it over."

She hesitated, then tossed her handbag on the desk. Eddie scooped it into a drawer. He put the gun in the drawer beside the bag.

"I don't have to introduce myself, do I?" he said.

She had recovered from the shock of seeing him. The color came back to her face. She moved to a chair and sat down. She crossed her legs, showing him her knees before adjusting her skirt.

"I know who you are," she said.

He took out a pack of cigarettes, got up and offered her a cigarette. She took it and he lit it. He sat on the edge of the desk close to her.

"What was the idea handing me your address and then yelling for the cops, baby?" he asked. "You nearly had me in trouble."

She let smoke drift down her nostrils. She didn't say anything.

"Don't act sullen, baby. You and me could get along fine together," he said.

"Could we?" Her blue eyes were cold. "Where's Frankie?"

"What makes you think I know where Frankie is?"

"You and Flynn met Frankie the night he disappeared. You met him at the filling station outside La Cygne. The boy there is a friend of mine. He called me. He said you and Flynn had guns. The next day, the boy was found shot through the head. Where's Frankie?"

Eddie was a little startled by this information. He saw now Ma had been smart to have thought of getting rid of the boy.

"I don't know, baby," he said. "I guess he's holed up some place. You should know more about him than I do." Anna continued to stare coldly at him. "What did you want to pull a gun on Frankie for?" she asked.

"Bailey was jumpy," Eddie said. "I didn't pull a gun, it was Flynn. There was nothing to it. He had the Blandish girl with him. I was a dope not to recognize her. If I had recognized her, I'd've taken her from Frankie, but I didn't. I've been kicking myself ever since. He told me she was a new girl friend and I fell for it. I let him drive away."

Two spots of red showed on Anna's cheeks and her eyes flashed angrily.

"I don't believe Frankie would walk out on me," she said. "I think something's happened to him and you know what it is."

"You're wrong, baby," Eddie said. "I'm just as much in the dark as you are, but I've got a few ideas."

"What ideas?"

"Forget it," he said, shaking his head. "Why rake over dirt? I know what the boys are saying, but they could be wrong."

"What are the boys saying?" Anna demanded, her eyes glittering.

"They say Riley's walked out on you. He's fallen for this Blandish girl."

Anna jumped to her feet.

"That's a lie! Frankie loves me! I know it's a lie."

"Sure, sure," Eddie said. "It could be, but where is he? Why hasn't he contacted you? When he lays his hands on the ransom, is he going to give you any of it? Doesn't look like it, does it?"

She began to move around the office. He could see he had undermined her confidence in Riley.

"That Blandish girl's a beauty," he went on. "You know it could be that Riley has ideas about her. You'd only be in the way if you were with him. I'm not so sure the boys are wrong about you and Riley. I guess he's taken you for a ride."

She confronted him.

"Shut up!" she shrilled. "Frankie wouldn't do a thing like that to me!"

"They all say that," Eddie said and moved over to look out of the window. He could see he had said enough. After a moment or so, she came over and stood by him.

"What am I going to do?" she said. "I haven't a dime."

"I'll lend you some money," Eddie said. "I like you, baby. How much do you want?"

"I wouldn't take money from you!"

"Okay, suit yourself. Any time you're short or in trouble, let me know. Pete'll tell you how to contact me. I've got to get moving. Forget Frankie. You're wasting your time thinking you'll hear from him. When he gets the ransom he'll have all the girls after him. So long, baby."

He went out of the office leaving Anna staring out of the window, tears scalding her eyes.

8

Flynn looked at his watch.

"Another five minutes," he said to Woppy who was nursing a Thompson machine gun. "Sweet Christ! I'll be goddamn glad when this caper's over."

"Yeah," Woppy said. "Still Ma says it's a cinch and she always knows what she's talking about"

"Then what the hell are you sweating for?" Flynn demanded.

The two men were sitting in the Buick which was drawn up by the side of the road in the shadows of a clump of shrubs. They had a clear view of the road ahead.

"You aren't so calm either," Woppy said, taking out a dirty handkerchief and mopping his face. "What's the time now?"

"Oh, shut up!" Flynn snarled. He was wishing Eddie had come with him. Woppy got on his nerves. With Eddie, he always felt if they got in a jam, they would get out of it, but Woppy was too excitable. He jumped off the deep end the moment anything started.

"I can hear a car," Woppy said.

In the distance, headlights appeared above the crest of the road.

"Here he comes!" Flynn said. He scrambled out of the car, pulling a powerful flashlight from his pocket.

The approaching car was traveling fast. When it was about

three hundred yards from Flynn, he started flashing the light.

Woppy watched, his hands clutching the machine gun, his heart hammering. Suppose the car was full of Feds, he thought. Those boys never took chances. They would storm past, spraying lead.

The approaching car slowed down. Flynn could see there was only the driver in the car. Blandish was obeying orders all right, he thought. The car swished past him. From the window a bulky object fell and thumped onto the road. The car went on, disappearing into the darkness.

Flynn blew out his cheeks. He ran to the white suitcase and picked it up.

Woppy put down the machine gun and started the car. Flynn scrambled in. He put the suitcase on the floor between his feet.

"Get going!" he said.

Woppy stepped on the gas pedal and the car surged forward. Flynn twisted around and stared through the rear window. They drove fast for three or four miles. No cars followed them.

"It's okay," Flynn said. "Let's get home."

When they walked into the sitting room, Ma, Slim, Eddie and Doc were all waiting. Flynn dumped the suitcase on the table.

"No trouble, Ma. It went like you said."

Ma got slowly to her feet and walked over to the table. She snapped back the twin locks of the suitcase. The others crowded around her. Even Slim seemed mildly excited.

She lifted the lid. They all stood staring at the neat packs of bills. They had never seen so much money in their lives.

"Man! Doesn't that look good!" Eddie said. "Man oh man!"

Slim hung over the money breathing heavily, his mouth hanging open.

"Well, there it is!" Ma said, trying to speak calmly. "A million dollars! At last!"

"Let's split it up, Ma," Eddie said. "I'm itching to spend some of my share. Come on! What's the split going to be?"

"Yeah," Woppy said, so excited he couldn't keep still. "What am I going to get, Ma?"

Ma closed the lid of the suitcase. She looked at each man

in turn, then she moved heavily to her armchair and sank into it.

The gang watched her, puzzled.

"What's biting you?" Eddie asked impatiently. "Let's have the money."

"Every one of those bills in that case has a number," Ma said. "You can bet your life the Feds have a list of the numbers. This money is so goddamn hot, it's on fire."

"What are you saying?" Eddie demanded, startled. "Can't we use the stuff?"

"Sure you can if you want a free ride to the gas chamber," Ma said. "I'm telling you it's suicide to spend it."

"Then what the hell did we get it for?" Flynn snarled.

Ma crackled.

"Okay, boys, relax. I've taken care of that angle. I'm trading this hot money to Schulberg. He's willing to sit on it for years, but in return we only get half a million. Still half a million of money you can use is better than a million you can't use."

Slim suddenly spat in the fireplace.

"Talk!" he said in disgust. "That's all you do. Talk!" He went over to the couch and lay down on it. He started to read the comics.

"That's not so hot, Ma," Eddie said. "I was expecting a split of two hundred grand."

Ma laughed.

"I dare say you were."

"What's the split then?" Woppy asked looking anxious.

"Each of you is getting three hundred dollars," Ma said, "and not a dollar more."

"You kidding? Three hundred bucks?" Eddie said, his face turning red. "What is this?"

"That's your spending money," Ma said. "Each of you is entitled to one hundred thousand dollars, but you're not getting it. I know you boys. If you got your hands on money that size, you'd make a splash that would put the Feds onto you in a week. You couldn't resist throwing your money around. That's the way most hoods get caught. They just can't resist flashing their bankroll and the Feds know it." She pointed her finger at Eddie. "What story would you tell the Feds if they asked you where you got all your sudden money from? Go on, tell me."

Eddie started to say something, then stopped. He was quick to see Ma was talking sense.

"You're right, Ma. This is a hell of a thing, isn't it? I thought I was going to be rich."

"Now I'll tell you what's going to happen to the money," Ma said. "We're going into business. For years now I've been wanting to go into business. You boys are going to handle it for me. I'm going to buy the Paradise Club. It's on the market. We'll redecorate it, get girls, a good band and we'll make money. With half a million bucks, we'll be able to turn the joint into something high class. I'm sick of running a small time gang. We're moving into big time. From now on, we're going to be in business. How do you like it?"

The four men relaxed. Slim was the only one who wasn't listening. He continued to read the comics.

Doc said, "You certainly got a brain in that head of yours, Ma. I'm for it."

"Me too," Eddie said. "It's a swell idea."

"Suits me," Flynn said.

"You going to have a restaurant, in the club, Ma?" Woppy asked. "Could I cook?"

Ma grinned.

"You can cook, Woppy. We each will own a fifth of the club's profits. You'll all be in the money and you'll have a reason for being in the money."

"Wait a minute," Eddie said. "Suppose the Feds want to know how you financed the deal. What then?"

"That's taken care of. Schulberg will say he lent me the money. That's part of the deal."

"You've certainly thought of everything," Eddie said. "When do we start, Ma?"

"Right away," Ma said. "The sooner the better. I'll buy the club tomorrow."

Flynn said, "And now there's the girl to be got rid of. Have you talked to Doc about her yet? And where are we going to bury her?"

The genial atmosphere exploded into pieces. Ma stiffened. She went white and then red. Doc's beaming smile slipped off his face. He looked as if he was going to faint. Slim dropped the newspaper and half sat up, his yellow eyes gleaming.

"Bury her?" Slim said. "What do you mean? Talk to Doc about what?" He swung his feet to the ground.

"Nothing," Ma said quickly. She looked as if she could kill Flynn.

Eddie decided this was the opportunity for a showdown.

"Just what is going to happen to the girl, Ma?" he asked, edging away from Slim who had got to his feet.

Ma hesitated, but she realized this was no time to back down. Without looking at Slim, she said, "She's got to go. She knows too much. When she's asleep..."

"Ma!"

Slim's voice, slightly high pitched, made them all look at him. He was glaring at his mother, his yellow eyes smouldering.

"What is it?" the old woman asked. She felt a chill of fear around her heart.

"She belongs to me," Slim said, speaking slowly and distinctly. "No one touches her unless they want to reckon with me first. She belongs to me and I'm keeping her."

"Look, Slim, don't be foolish," Ma said. She spoke with difficulty. Her mouth felt dry. "We can't keep her. It's too dangerous. She's got to go."

Slim suddenly kicked a chair out of his way. His knife jumped into his hand. Woppy and Doc hurriedly backed away from Ma, leaving her to face Slim alone. She stiffened as Slim began slowly to move towards her.

"Then you'll reckon with me," he said viciously. "Do you want me to cut your throat, you old cow? If you touch her—if anyone touches her—I'll cut you to pieces!"

Eddie slid his gun into his hand. Ma saw the move.

"Put that gun up!" she said hoarsely. She was terrified Eddie was going to shoot her son.

Slim turned on Eddie who backed away.

"You hear me?" Slim screamed. "She's mine! I'm keeping her! No one's touching her!"

He stared around at each of them in turn, then he went out, slamming the door behind him.

There was a long pause. Ma was pale. She went slowly to her chair and sat down. She looked suddenly old.

Eddie and Flynn exchanged glances. Eddie shrugged and made for the door. Flynn followed him out of the room.

Woppy, sweating, sat on the couch and pretended to look at the comics. Doc poured himself a stiff drink. The silence in the room was painful.

Slim stood at the head of the stairs, listening. He grinned to himself. At last he had shown his power. He had scared them all. From now on, he was going to have his rightful place in the gang. Ma was going to take second place. He looked down the passage at Miss Blandish's room. It was time he stopped sitting by her night after night. He must show her he wasn't only master of his mother, but master of her too.

He started down the passage, his yellow eyes gleaming. He took the key out of the lock after unlocking the door. He went into the room and locked the door.

Miss Blandish watched him come across the room. She saw his new confidence and she guessed what it was to mean to her.

Shuddering, she shut her eyes.

CHAPTER THREE

1

Across the frosted panel of the door ran the legend:
DAVE FENNER. INVESTIGATIONS.

The lettering was in black and recently painted.

The door led into a small, well-furnished office with a desk, two lounging chairs, a good Oriental carpet and wall shelves full of law books recently acquired and never opened.

David Fenner lounged in the desk chair, his feet on the desk. He was staring blankly up at the ceiling. He had the air of a man with nothing to do and all the time in the world to do it in.

Fenner was a massively built man of thirty-three. He was dark, with an attractively ugly face and a pugnacious jaw of a man who likes to get his own way and generally does.

A door to the left of the desk led into the outer office. A wooden barrier divided this room. One side was reserved for waiting clients; the other side was the general office presided over by, Paula Dolan, an attractive girl with raven black wavy hair, large suggestive blue eyes and a figure that Fenner declared was the only asset of value in the newly established business.

Paula sat before an idle typewriter, thumbing through the pages of a lurid magazine called *Love*. From time to time, she yawned and her eyes continually strayed to the wall clock. The time was twenty minutes after three.

The buzzer sounded on her desk, making her start. She put down the magazine and walked into the inner office.

"Got any cigarettes, honey?" Fenner asked, hunching his muscles so the chair creaked. "I'm all out."

"I've got three left," Paula said. "You can have two of them." She went into her office and returned with two cigarettes which she laid on the table.

"That's pretty generous of you," Fenner said, lighting up. "Thanks." He inhaled deeply while he looked Paula over. "That's a nice shape you've got on your bones this afternoon."

"Yes, isn't it?" Paula said bitterly. "It doesn't seem to get me anywhere."

"How are you making out?" Fenner said, quick to change the subject. "Got anything to do?"

"As much as you have," Paula said, hoisting herself up on the desk.

"Then you sure must be working yourself to death," Fenner said, grinning. "Never mind: something'll turn up."

"You've been saying just that for the past month," Paula said. She looked worried. "We can't go on much longer like this, Dave. The Office Equipment people telephoned. Unless you pay the third installment on the furniture by tomorrow, they want it all back."

Fenner surveyed the room.

"You don't say! You wouldn't think anyone in their right minds would want this junk back, would you?"

"Perhaps you didn't hear what I said," Paula said ominously. "They'll take all the furniture away tomorrow unless you pay the third installment. So what shall I have to sit on?"

Fenner looked startled.

"They're not taking *that* away as well, are they?"

"Dave Fenner, will you never be serious for half a minute? If we don't find two hundred dollars by tomorrow morning, we will have to shut down."

Fenner sighed.

"Money! How much have we got?"

"Ten dollars and fifteen cents."

"As much as that?" he waved his hand airily. "Why, we're rich! There's a guy across the way who's got nothing but an overdraft."

"How does that make us rich?" Paula demanded.

"Well, we don't owe the bank money."

"That's not your fault. You've tried hard enough to owe them money, haven't you?"

"I guess that's right." Fenner shook his head mournfully. "I don't think those birds trust me."

"Oh, no," Paula said sarcastically. "They just don't want to embarrass you." She patted a stray curl into place. "I'm beginning to think you made a mistake opening this office. You were making good money on the *Tribune*. I never did think this agency idea of yours would work out." Fenner looked indignant.

"Well, that's a fine thing to say. Then why did you quit your job and come to work for me? I warned you it could be tough at the start, but nothing short of a machine gun would stop you joining me." Paula smiled at him.

"Maybe it was because I love you," she said softly Fenner groaned.

"For the love of Mike, don't start that all over again. I've enough worries without you adding to them. Why don't you get smart, honey? A girl with your looks and your shape could hook a millionaire. Why waste your time and talents on a loser like me? I'll tell you something: I'll always be broke. It's a tradition in the family. My grandfather was a bankrupt. My father was a pauper. My uncle was a miser: he went crazy because he couldn't find any money to mise over."

"When are we going to get married, Dave?"

"Remind me to consult my ouija board sometime," Fenner said hurriedly. "Why don't you go home? You're getting unhealthy ideas sticking around here with nothing to do. Take the afternoon off. Go shampoo your hair or something."

Paula lifted her shoulders in resigned helplessness. "Why don't you talk to Ryskind? He might give you your job back if you asked him nicely. You were the best crime reporter in the game, Dave. He must miss you. Why don't you talk to him?" Fenner shook his head.

"The trouble there is he wouldn't talk to me. I called him a double-crossing, stony-hearted, brainless moron just before I quit. I also seem to remember I told him if ever he invited me to his parents' wedding. I wouldn't go. Somehow, I don't think he likes me any more."

A buzzer sounded in the outer office announcing a visitor. "Who do you imagine that could be?" Fenner asked, frowning.

"Probably the man to disconnect the telephone," Paula said. "We haven't paid the bill—remember?"

"What do we want a telephone for?" Fenner asked. "We're not on speaking terms with anyone in town, are we?"

Paula went into the outer office, closing the door after her. In a couple of minutes, she was back, her face alight with excitement.

"Look who's here!" she said and laid a card on his blotter.
Fenner read the card, then he sat back, gaping at Paula.
"John Blandish! In person?"
"He wants to see you."
"You're sure it's him, not someone impersonating him?"
"I'm sure."
"Well, what are you waiting for? Shoo him in, baby; shoo him in!"
Paula went to the door and opened it.
"Mr. Fenner is free now, Mr. Blandish. Would you come in?"
She stood aside as John Blandish entered the room, then she went out, leaving the two men together.
Fenner got to his feet. He was surprised Blandish wasn't a bigger man. Only slightly above middle height, the millionaire seemed puny beside Fenner's muscular bulk. His eyes gave his face its arresting power and character. They were hard, shrewd and alert eyes of a man who has fought his way to the top with no mercy asked nor given.
Blandish gave Fenner a quick critical look as the two men shook hands.
"I have a proposition for you, Fenner," Blandish said. "I think you're the man I'm looking for. I hear you have connections with the underworld. I believe the only way to bring to justice the men who kidnapped my daughter, is to employ someone like you who can freelance among the mobs with no restrictions. What do you think?"
"I think you're right," Fenner said, sitting down behind his desk. "Anyway, the theory's right, but your daughter was kidnapped three months ago. The trail's pretty cold now."
"I am aware of that," Blandish said. He took out a pigskin cigar case and selected a cigar. "I had to give the Federal Agents every chance of finding these men before I started interfering. Well, they haven't found them. Now I'm going to try. I've talked to them and I've talked to the Police. It was Captain Brennan who suggested I should contact you. He tells me you have a good reputation as a newspaper man and wide connections among the thugs in this City. He said if I employed you, he would cooperate with you to the best of his ability. I'm prepared to give you the opportunity of finding these men if you are interested. I will pay you three thousand dollars right now and

if you find them, you'll get a further thirty thousand dollars. That's my proposition. What do you say?"

Fenner sat for a moment slightly stunned, then pulling himself together, he nodded.

"I'll certainly have a try, Mr. Blandish, but I'm not promising to deliver. The F.B.I. are the best in the world. If they've failed to find these hoods, I'll probably fail too, but I'll have a try."

"How do you propose to start?"

"It so happened I covered the kidnapping for the *Tribune*," Fenner said. "It was the last job I did before leaving the paper. I've got a file covering all the facts. This I want to study. One thing has always struck me as odd. I knew both Riley and Bailey personally. I was continually running into them in dives and clubs when I was checking for information during the course of my work. They were strictly small time. How they ever found the nerve to go through with the kidnapping beats me, and yet, apparently they did. It doesn't make sense. If you knew the hoodlums the way I know them, you'd feel the same way about these two. Kidnapping is out of character. The most they would ever aspire to is a small bank holdup. Anyway, there it is. They kidnapped your daughter. Then I ask myself how could they have vanished into thin air? How is it none of the ransom money has ever appeared? What are these kidnappers living on if they aren't spending the ransom? Another thing; Riley had a girl friend: Anna Borg. The Federal Agents spent hours questioning her, but they didn't get a thing out of her. I know for a fact Riley was crazy about her and yet he just walked out of her life as if she never existed. It doesn't add up." He paused, then went on, "I'll see Brennan right away, Mr. Blandish. I'll go through the file to make sure I've missed nothing there that might give me a lead. In a couple of days I'll be able to tell you if I think I have a chance or not of finding these men." He looked searchingly at Mr. Blandish. "You don't ask me to find your daughter. You think...?"

Blandish's face hardened.

"She is dead. I have no doubt about that. It would be an impossible thought to think of her still alive and in the hands of such men. No, she's dead." He took from his pocket a checkbook and wrote out a check to Fenner for three thousand dollars.

"Then I expect to hear from you in two days' time?"

"That's right."

Fenner went with Blandish to the door.

"Money is no object," Blandish said. "I'm not restricting you. Get among the underworld and let them know there's money to be had for talking. I'm sure it's the only way to get the lead we want."

"You leave it to me," Fenner said. "I'll try not to disappoint you."

When Blandish had gone, Paula came rushing into the room.

"What did he want?" she asked anxiously. "Has he hired you?"

Fenner showed her the check.

"We're in the money, sweetheart," he said. "Here, take a look. Three thousand bucks! Saved in the nick of time! You can relax. You've still got a chair to park your fanny on."

2

Captain Charles Brennan, City Police, a fat, red-faced man with blue hard eyes and sandy-colored hair, greying at the temples, reached across his desk to shake hands with Fenner.

"Never thought the day would come when I would be glad to see a detective in my office," he said. "Sit down. How's tricks?"

"Could be worse," Fenner said, sitting down. "I'm not the grumbling kind."

"I was surprised to hear you had applied for a licence to operate as an investigator," Brennan said, lighting a cigar. "You should have stuck to newspaper work. A detective's life isn't fit for a dog."

"I don't aim to live as well as a dog," Fenner said, cheerfully. "Thanks for the introduction to Blandish."

Brennan waved his hand airily.

"Between me and you and my aunt's wooden leg, Blandish has been gradually driving me nuts. With any luck now, he'll drive you nuts and lay off me."

Fenner stiffened to attention.

"What do you mean?"

"You wait," Brennan said with sadistic relish. "Blandish

hasn't got off my neck since his goddamn daughter was snatched. In self-defense I had to suggest he should hire you. Morning, noon and night he was either here in my office or on the telephone. When was I going to find the men who kidnapped his daughter? If I heard that once, I've heard it a thousand times. Those words, when I'm dead, will be found engraved on my liver!"

"Well, that's pretty nice," Fenner said bitterly, "and I was thinking you were doing me a good turn."

"I'm no boy scout," Brennan said. "I'll tell you this much: you have as much chance of finding those punks as you have of winning a beauty prize."

Fenner let that ride.

"But they must be somewhere."

"Sure, they're somewhere. They could be in Mexico, Canada, heaven or hell. Every policeman in the world has been looking for them for three months—not a sign, but I agree with you, they must be somewhere."

"How about the girl? Do you think she's dead?"

"Yeah. She must be dead. Why should they keep her alive? She would only be a danger to them. I wouldn't mind betting they knocked her off when they killed MacGowan, but where they buried her beats me."

"How about Anna Borg?" Fenner asked. "What became of her?"

"She's still around. I've had one of my boys trailing her for the past two months, but it's a waste of time. She has a new boy friend now. I guess she got tired of waiting for Riley to show up. She's doing an act now at the Paradise Club."

"Who's the new boy friend?"

"Eddie Schultz."

Fenner frowned, then he snapped his fingers.

"I know him, one of the Grisson gang; a tall, big, good-looking punk."

"That's him. The Grisson gang have taken over the Paradise Club: a down-at-the-heel joint run by an Italian:

Toni Rocco. They bought him out, put money in the joint and it's quite a club now."

Fenner looked interested.

"Where did the money come from? The Grisson gang weren't

in the dough, were they?"

"I checked all that," Brennan said, looking wise. "Abe Schulberg is financing the club. He's done a deal with Ma Grisson. She runs the club and gives him a fifty percent cut."

Fenner lost interest. He lit a cigarette, sliding down in his chair.

"So the trail's cold?"

"It never was hot. It's a bitch of a case. The time and money we've wasted on it gives me nightmares. We're no closer to a solution than when we first started."

Fenner pulled a face. The vision of laying his hands on thirty thousand dollars now began to look remote. He got to his feet. Then a thought struck him.

"What did this Borg girl do for a living when she was going around with Riley?" he asked.

"She did a strip act at the Cosmos Club, strictly for peanuts, but her main meal ticket was Riley."

"The Cosmos Club?" Fenner suddenly looked thoughtful. He glanced at his watch. "Well, I'm wasting your time, Captain. If I turn up anything, I'll let you know."

"You won't," Brennan said, grinning. "There's nothing to turn up."

In a thoughtful mood, Fenner drove back to his office. He found Paula waiting for him although it was after six o'clock.

"You still here?" he said as he entered the office. "Haven't you a home to go to?"

"I'm scared to leave in case another millionaire walks in," Paula said, her blue eyes wide. "Oh, Dave! I've been planning how we'll spend all that beautiful money when we get it"

"The operative word in that pipe dream of a sentence of yours is when." Fenner walked into his office. Paula trailed after him. "Since you are still working, baby, make yourself useful. Check the dirty file and see if we have anything on Pete Cosmos."

During the years Fenner had been a newspaperman, he had systematically collected every scrap of information concerning the activities of the big and little gangsters in town. He had collected an enormous library of facts that often came in handy when he was trying to persuade some hood to give him information.

In five minutes, Paula came into the office with a pile of newspaper clippings.

"I don't know what you're looking for, Dave," she said, "but here's everything we have on Cosmos."

"Thanks, sweetheart, now you trot off home. I've got work to do. How would you like to have dinner with me tonight to celebrate our riches?"

Paula's face lit up with delighted surprise.

"I'd love it! I'll wear my new dress! Let's go to the Champagne Room! I've never been there. I hear it's a knockout."

"The only knockout about that joint is the check," Fenner said. "Maybe we might go there when we have got our hooks into the thirty thousand, but not before."

"Then how about the Astor? For the money, they say it's the best in town."

"Don't be simple, baby. They didn't say for how much money, did they?" Fenner put his arm around her coaxingly. "I'll tell you where we'll go, the Cosmos Club. We'll combine business with pleasure."

Paula made a grimace as if she had bitten into a lemon.

"The Cosmos Club? That joint's not even a dive and the food's poisonous."

"Run along, baby, I've work to do. I'll pick you up at eight-thirty at your place," and turning her, Fenner gave her a slap on her behind, launching her fast to the door.

He sat down at his desk and began to read through the mass of clippings Paula had given him. After some thirty minutes, he made a telephone call, then he put the clippings back into the filing cabinet, turned off the lights in the office, locked up and went down to his car. He drove to his two room apartment where he took a shower and changed into a dark suit. He checked his .38 police special and put it in his shoulder holster.

He found Paula anxiously waiting for him. One of the important facts of life that Paula had learned the hard way was not to keep any man waiting. She was looking cute in a black dress, relieved by a red carnation. The cut of the dress accentuated her figure so that Fenner took a second look.

"What kills me," Paula said as she got into the car with a generous show of nylon-clad legs, "is I always have to buy my own corsage. The day you think of buying me one, I'll faint."

"Put your smelling salts away, baby," Fenner said, grinning.
"I would never think of it. You haven't a worry in the world." He
edged the car into the traffic. "I've got something on Pete. Boy!
Won't his fat face turn red when I start talking to him."

Paula looked at him.

"I hope we'll eat sometime," she said. "I foresee you and that
fat Italian sitting glaring at each other and grinding your teeth
while I starve to death."

"We'll eat first, baby," Fenner said and patted her knee.

She firmly removed his hand.

"That knee is reserved for my future husband," she said.
"You can have an option on it if you want it, but it'll have to be
in writing."

Fenner laughed. He liked going out with Paula. They always
seemed to have fun together.

The Cosmos Club was full when they arrived, but the *maitre
d'hotel*, a seedy, narrow-eyed Italian, found them a table.

Fenner looked around and decided it was a pretty crummy
joint. He hadn't been in the club for six months. He could see it
had changed for the worse.

"Charming little morgue," Paula said, looking around. "I
can't imagine anyone coming here unless they were too mean to
go somewhere else."

Fenner let that one ride. He was studying the menu. He was
hungry. A grubby looking waiter hovered at his side.

After a long discussion they decided on the iced melon, and
duck cooked with olives to follow.

"At least we can eat the olives," Paula said. "Even the cook
at the Cosmos Club can't spoil olives."

Fenner laughed.

"You wait and see. I bet you they'll be as tender as golf
balls."

But when the meal was served, neither of them could
complain. It wasn't good, but at least they could eat it.

Between courses, they danced. Paula attempted to get
romantic, but Fenner deliberately trod on her toes. The dancing
wasn't a success.

While she was choosing dessert, Fenner pushed back his
chair and stood up.

"Business now, baby," he said. "I'm going to talk to Pete. You go ahead and stuff yourself. I won't be long."

Paula smiled at him, her eyes furious.

"Go ahead, Dave darling, don't worry about me. I have lots and lots to talk to myself about. I'll expect you when I don't see you."

"If we weren't in a public place," Fenner said, stung, "I would put you over my knee and slap you humpbacked."

"A charming thought," Paula said, waving him away. "Run along and talk to your friend. I hope he spits in your right eye."

Grinning, Fenner made his way to Pete's office. He didn't bother to knock. He walked right in and kicked the door shut behind him.

Pete was adding up figures in a ledger. He looked up, startled. When he saw who it was, he scowled.

"Who told you to bust in here?" he demanded. "What do you want?"

"Hello, fatty," Fenner said coming over and sitting on the desk. "Long time no see."

"What do you want?" Pete asked again, glaring at Fenner.

"Have you seen Harry Levane recently?"

Pete stiffened.

"No, and I don't want to. Why?"

"I've just been talking to him. Pete, you are in bad trouble." Fenner shook his head sadly. "Harry was telling me about the girl you took to Miami last summer. She was a minor. Pete! I'm surprised at you! You stand to get a two-year stretch for that little indiscretion."

Pete looked as if someone had driven a needle into his behind.

"It's a lie!" he shouted, his face white. "I don't know what you're talking about!"

Fenner smiled pityingly at him.

"Don't be a chump, Pete. Harry saw you with her. He hasn't forgotten you got him three years for the Clifford jewel steal. He's aching to put you away."

Pete's face broke out in a sweat.

"I'll kill the punk! He can't prove it!"

"He can. He knows who the girl is and he's talked to her. She's ready to sign a complaint."

Pete slumped back in his chair.

"Where is she?" he said, his voice husky. "I'll talk to her. I'll fix it. Where is she?"

"I know where she is. I know where Harry is. It'll cost you, Pete, but what's money," Fenner said. "But I'm not telling you if we can't do a deal. I want information. I'll trade what you want for what I want."

Pete glared at him.

"What do you want?"

"Nothing to it, Pete; just a little information. Do you remember Anna Borg?"

Pete looked surprised.

"Yes—what about her?'

"She worked here?"

"That's right."

"Did she ever hint that she knew where Riley was hiding out?"

"She didn't know. I'll swear to that."

"She did mention Riley?"

"I'll say! She was swearing and cursing about him all the time."

"How did she meet Schultz?"

Pete hesitated.

"This is a trade? You tell me where I contact that little bitch and Harry?"

"It's a trade."

"Schultz came here a few days after the snatch," Pete said. "He wanted to know how he could contact Anna. He said Ma Grisson wanted to talk to the girl. When I told him the Feds were watching Anna, he told me to call her and get her down here in this office. I wasn't here when they met, but a couple of days later, Anna quit working for me. She said she had been offered a better job. When the Grissons took over the Paradise Club, she started working there. Eddie and she are living together."

"Why was Ma Grisson interested in the girl?" Fenner asked.

Pete shrugged his shoulders.

"I don't know."

Fenner got to his feet. He bent over the desk and scribbled two addresses on a scratch pad.

"There you are," he said. "I'd contact those two fast. Harry is aching to see you in jail. It'll cost you plenty to keep his mouth shut."

As Pete reached for the telephone, Fenner made his way back to the restaurant.

He found Paula talking animatedly to a slim, handsome gigolo who was leaning over her, looking with interest down the front of her dress.

Fenner gave him a heavy nudge.

"Okay, buster, set sail and fade away."

The gigolo looked quickly at Fenner's massive shoulders and his pugnacious jaw and he hurriedly backed away.

"Don't let this ape worry you," Paula said. "Brush him off. One good smack in the jaw will fix him."

But the gigolo was already in retreat halfway across the room.

"Hi, baby, I'm surprised at the company you keep," Fenner said, smiling at her.

Paula leaned back in her chair and smiled at him.

"Did your Italian friend spit in your eye?"

"No, but that doesn't mean he didn't want to. Come on, baby. I want to go to bed."

She looked interested.

"Alone?"

"Yeah, alone," Fenner said, piloting her out of the restaurant. "I want all my strength for tomorrow. I'm calling on Anna Borg and from what I hear, she's more than a handful."

Paula got into the car and straightened her skirt.

"Isn't she a stripper?"

"Yeah," Fenner said and grinned. "Don't look so prim; just because she is, I don't have to be one of that fan dancer's fans."

3

Chief of Police Brennan had been right when he had told Fenner that the Grisson gang had taken over the Paradise Club, but he had been wrong when he had said the gang had bought out the owner, Toni Rocco.

Rocco had been ruthlessly squeezed out.

Ma Grisson with Eddie and Flynn had called on Rocco and had explained just why it would be more healthy for him to hand the club over to her and accept her generous offer of one percent of the profits.

At one time Rocco had been a successful jockey. He was a tiny man and Ma's vast, menacing presence frightened him. Although he didn't make much money out of his club, bought from his horse racing savings, he was proud of it. To give it up was to give up his dearest possession, but he was smart enough to know if he didn't give it up, he wouldn't last long and Rocco wasn't ready to die just yet.

Ma saw no reason why she should spend good money for the club when she knew she could get it for nothing. Although she had now a half a million dollars to play with, the structural alterations she had in mind, the furnishings, the kitchen equipment, the mirrors and the lighting would cost plenty. She told Rocco a one-percent cut on the profits was fair and generous and she waved aside his muttered protest that a five-percent cut would be more acceptable.

"Use your head, my friend," she said, smiling her wolfish smile. "One percent of anything is better than nothing. There's a bunch of tough boys who have had their eyes on this club for some time. Before long they will shake you down for protection. Once they start on you, they'll bleed you white. If you don't pay, one of them will plant a bomb in here. If we take over the club, they'll fade away. They know it wouldn't be safe to threaten us."

Rocco knew very well there were no tough boys, but he was also sure if he didn't surrender the club, one of the Grisson gang would plant a bomb on him.

So he signed away his rights to the club with deceptive humility. The partnership agreement that Ma's attorney drew up was a complicated document that said a lot and meant nothing. Rocco hadn't even the right to check the books. Whatever came to him came as a favor. He had a shrewd idea that his cut of the profits wouldn't be worth the trouble to collect.

Ma Grisson was very satisfied with the transaction, but she might not have been so satisfied had she known that Rocco had promised himself that he would settle his account with the Grisson gang. Sooner or later, he told himself, an opportunity must arise, and when it did, the old bitch would regret having done what she had done to him.

Because of his apparent mildness and his size, no one,

least of all Ma Grisson, realized what a dangerous enemy Rocco could be. Behind the dark, thin Italian features, there dwelt a cunning, ruthless and vicious mentality.

Rocco got himself a job as a collector for the local numbers racket. He didn't like the job, but he had to earn a living now that he had lost the club. As he walked the streets, entering shabby apartments, climbing stairs until his legs ached, he brooded about the Grisson gang. Sooner or later, he kept promising himself he would fix them and when he did fix them, they would stay fixed.

Ma Grisson had selected the Paradise Club not only because she could get it for nothing but also because of its convenient position.

The two-storied building stood in a small courtyard off one of the main avenues. It was sandwiched between a warehouse and a clock factory: both these buildings were deserted between six p.m. and eight a.m.

The club building was so situated that in the event of a police raid, the doorman would have ample time to sound the warning bell. The building was impossible to surround.

One of the first things Ma ordered was a three-inch thick steel door with a judas window made of bulletproof glass. This door took the place of the previous door to the entrance of the club. All the windows of the building were fitted with steel shutters which could slam shut at the touch of a button on Ma's desk.

In a surprisingly short time, Ma had converted the club into a fortress. She had constructed a secret staircase that led from the upper floor into the basement of the adjacent warehouse. Unknown to the owner of the warehouse, it was now possible to enter and leave the club unseen through the warehouse.

The decor of the club had been executed by an expensive but clever decorator. The reception hall was in white and gilt with rose-colored mirrors. To the right was the restaurant and dance floor, designed to resemble a vast cave with stalactites hanging from the ceiling and niches around the room for favored customers who wished to see, but not to be seen. The room was lit by green fluorescent tubes that cast an intriguing but ghostly light, creating an atmosphere at once decadent and neurotic.

At the far end of the restaurant, guarded by another three-inch thick steel door was the gambling room with roulette and baccarat tables. Leading from the gambling room was Ma's office and another room used by the gang to entertain their own special friends.

Upstairs were six bedrooms for the use of high paying customers who wanted relaxation with their girl friends without the necessity of leaving the club. At the far end of the corridor was a locked door leading to Miss Blandish's suite.

Two months after Ma Grisson had squeezed Rocco out of business, the club was reopened and became an immediate hit.

The cave restaurant was the talk of the town. It was the fashionable thing to become a member of the club, and here Ma showed her genius for running a club. She announced in the press that the membership was strictly limited to 300 members. The entrance fee was three hundred dollars. There was an immediate rush of applicants. Had she wished, Ma could have had over five thousand members within a week of opening. Refusing to be tempted, and resisting the pressure of the other members of the gang who yelled to her to take the suckers' money, she selected three hundred names from the mass of names sent in, carefully choosing only the most influential and wealthy members of Kansas City's society.

"This way," she told the gang, "we get class. I know what I'm doing. I don't want a lot of hoodlums in here, making trouble. This joint is going to be the best in town; you wait and see."

Both Flynn and Woppy were intimidated by the grandeur of the club. Woppy was scared to go into the kitchens where three chefs, bribed away from the best hotels in the City, presided. His dream of being head cook evaporated at the sight of these experts in their high chef's caps and their trained, efficient methods.

Doc Williams was delighted with the club. It gave him tremendous satisfaction to wear a tuxedo and act the genial host at the bar where he drank himself into happy oblivion night after night.

Eddie was also pleased with the club. He ran the gambling room while Flynn kept an eye on the restaurant. Ma seldom put in an appearance. She remained in her office, handling the catering, the books and the money.

The one fish completely out of water was Slim. He still crept about looking dirty and disheveled. He still wore the greasy black suit he had worn for years. He kept away from the activities of the club, spending most of his time with Miss Blandish.

He had insisted that Miss Blandish should have not only a bedroom but also a sitting room. Ma had let him have his way. Having the girl on the premises worried her. She was well aware of the risk they were all running, having the girl there. Miss Blandish was the only surviving evidence that the Grisson gang had done the kidnapping. If ever she was found there, all Ma's hopes, her plans for the future would go up in smoke. She hoped before long that Slim would get bored with the girl. When that happened, Ma would get rid of her.

While Fenner and Paula were driving home, the Paradise Club was just coming alive.

Maisey, the hat check girl, was busy taking wraps, hats and coats from the steady stream of arriving customers. Maisey, hired by Ma because of her outrageous figure, was a sable-haired teenager with a vapid, characterless prettiness, a docile attitude towards exploring male hands, and an eye for the fast buck.

Her working uniform consisted of a scarlet, tight fitting jacket and white satin shorts. Her long attractive legs were in black net tights and on her head was perched a white pillbox, cocked over one saucy eye.

Maisey was responsible for two jobs: to look after the cloakrooms and to see no unauthorized person went upstairs.

For some minutes she worked hard and fast, then there was a lull in the arrivals and for a moment or so the lobby was empty.

She saw Slim come in, carrying a brown paper parcel.

Slim gave Maisey the creeps. She hurriedly turned her back on him, pretending to straighten the line of coats and wraps so she could avoid looking at him.

Slim went up the stairs and along the passage to Miss Blandish's room. He paused outside the door to look back along the passage, then taking out a key, he unlocked the door and entered the big, airy sitting room.

Every time he entered the room, he liked it better. He had never seen such a beautiful room. Decorated in grey and blue, furnished with grey leather lounging chairs, a blue carpet and a big television set, it was to him, the most wonderful room in the world. The only thing it lacked was windows, but even Slim realized it would have been too dangerous to keep the girl in a room with windows.

He walked into the bedroom and paused in the doorway.

This room he liked as well as the sitting room. It was decorated in off-white and rose. The large double bed dominated the room with its rose quilted head board. There was another big television set at the end of the bed. Slim was a television addict. He never grew tired of watching the moving pictures on the twenty-one inch screen.

Miss Blandish sat before the dressing table. She had on a rose-colored wrap which had fallen open to show her long, beautiful legs. Her bare feet were thrust into rose-colored mules. She was manicuring her nails lifelessly, and although she heard Slim come in, she didn't look up.

"Hello," Slim said. "I've got a present for you." He moved over to her. "You're lucky. No one gives me presents."

Miss Blandish laid down the nail file and dropped her hands in her lap. There was a blank, hypnotized expression on her face that now constantly irritated Slim.

"It cost a lot of money," Slim said, watching her closely to see if she was listening. "But money means nothing to me now. I can buy you anything I want. I have all the money in the world. Look—what do you think this is?" He pushed the parcel toward her, but Miss Blandish ignored it. Muttering, Slim put his cold, damp hand on her arm and pinched her flesh. She didn't move. She grimaced and closed her eyes. "Wake up!" Slim said angrily. "What's the matter with you? Here, open the parcel."

The drugged girl made a feeble attempt to untie the string, but seeing her fumbling, Slim snatched the parcel away from her.

"I'll do it! I like opening packages." He began to unknot the string. "You seen Ma today?"

"No." Miss Blandish spoke hesitatingly. "I haven't seen her."

"She doesn't like you. She wants to get rid of you. If it wasn't for me, you'd be at the bottom of the river by now. You don't know how well off you are. When I was a kid, I saw them take a woman out of the river. She was all blown up. One of the cops vomited. I didn't. I wanted to see, but they drove me away. She had hair just like yours." He suddenly lost patience with the string and pulling out his knife, he cut the string, tearing off the paper. "It's a picture. It's pretty. When I saw it, I thought of you." He examined the small oil painting, smiling at it. There was no form to the picture, but the colors were hard and violent. "Do you like it?" He thrust the picture at Miss Blandish who stared sightlessly at it and then looked away.

There was a long pause while Slim stared at her. There were moments, Slim found himself thinking, when he wished this girl wasn't a puppet. Now after three months when he had done everything his perverted mind could devise to her, her drugged lack of resistance began to pall. He would have liked some opposition. He would have liked her to struggle against his advances so that he could exercise his talent for cruelty.

"Don't you like it?" he demanded, glaring at her. "It cost a lot of money. Say something, can't you? Don't sit there staring like a goddamn dummy! Say something!"

Miss Blandish shuddered. She got up and went over to the bed. She lay down, covering her face with her hands.

Slim looked at the picture. He suddenly hated it.

"It cost a hundred bucks," he said viciously. "Do you think I care? If you don't like it—say so! I can buy you something else!" He suddenly slashed the canvas with his knife, hacking and slashing while he poured out a stream of filthy curses. "Now you're not having it!" he shouted, flinging the ruined picture across the room. "I'm too good to you. You want to suffer! People who have never suffered, never appreciate anything!" He got up and went over to her. "You hear me? You ought to suffer!"

Miss Blandish lay still, her eyes closed. She might have been dead.

Slim bent over her. He pricked her throat with the tip of his knife.

"I could kill you," he snarled. "Do you hear? I could kill you."

She opened her eyes and looked at him. A spot of blood appeared on her white skin where the knife had cut her. Her dazed, enlarged pupils sickened him. He drew away. She wasn't his, he was thinking; he was kidding himself. She was nothing—a dead body. His mind switched to Ma and Doc. They were responsible. He fingered his knife. They had spoiled his pleasure. They had turned his beautiful picture-book dream into a lifeless nightmare.

Muttering to himself, he went into the sitting room. He turned on the television. In a few seconds he was staring with fixed attention at the picture of a man and a woman passionately embracing.

Among the customers who came in a steady stream into the reception lobby was a short, stockily built man wearing a tuxedo that didn't quite fit him.

Eddie, lounging by the cloakroom, eyed this man suspiciously. Eddie thought he looked like a cop and as soon the man had entered the restaurant, Eddie went down the doorman, a husky bouncer named MacGowan.

"Who was that bird?" Eddie asked. "He looked like a cop."

"He's been in here before," MacGowan said. "Mr. Williams brought him in. Mr. Williams said if he came alone, we could let him in."

Harry Williams was one of the club's biggest spenders. All the same Eddie decided he'd better have a word with Ma.

He found her in her office, busy as usual with a mass of papers.

"What is it?" she demanded. "I'm busy."

"Guy just came in who looks like a cop," Eddie said. "He signed in as Jay Doyle. Mac says he's been here before as H.W.'s guest."

"Don't tell me, tell the boys," she said impatiently. "Don't be so goddamn helpless. You know what to do. Make sure he doesn't get into the gambling room or upstairs."

Eddie hurried down to the restaurant. He entered as the band leader was introducing the first cabaret act. Eddie spotted Doyle sitting alone in one of the dark corners. He couldn't see Flynn so he decided he would watch Doyle himself.

"Well, folks," the bandleader was saying, "this is the moment you have all been waiting for. Once again Miss Anna Borg presents yet another of her famous—or should I say infamous—passion dances. A big hand for Miss Borg, if you please."

While the clapping started up, the drummer ran off a roll and the lights went out. A white spotlight centered on the middle of the dance floor. Out of the darkness, Anna appeared.

Eddie grinned. He had certainly been smart when he had picked Anna for his sidekick. He had had a lot of trouble with her, grooming her, helping her work up her act, but now it was paying off. Even Ma had admitted Anna was the big attraction at the club.

Anna swept into the glare of the spotlight. She had on a gold lame dress with a long zipper down the front. The band started the old favorite "Can't help lovin' that Man." Anna's voice was hard and loud. As she sang she slowly pulled down the zipper, then suddenly stepped out of the dress, tossing it to a waiting page boy who was leering at her and winking into the darkness.

Dressed now in white bra and panties, she continued to sing. The customers didn't bother about her singing: they feasted their eyes on her body contortions.

At the end of the first chorus, she discarded her bra. At the end of the second chorus she took off her panties. Wearing only a G-string, she began to circle the tables, while the spotlight chased her.

She's hot, Eddie thought, watching her bowing and blowing kisses at the end of her song. The customers loved her. She had slid into her dress now and the lights had come up.

Eddie glanced across the room to where Doyle had been sitting. He stiffened. Under cover of the darkness, Doyle had disappeared.

4

Fenner was having his morning coffee when the front door bell rang. Wondering who it could be at this hour, he went to the door.

A short stockily built man grinned cheerfully at him.

"I'm Jay Doyle," he said. "City police. Too early for you?"

"Come on in. I'm just having coffee," Fenner said.

"The Captain told me to call on you," Doyle said, tossing his hat on a chair and sitting down. "He tells me you are representing Blandish now."

Fenner poured a second cup of coffee.

"That's the idea. Sugar?"

"No, thanks." Doyle lit a cigarette. "For the past two months I've been tailing the Borg girl. There was just a chance Riley would have got in touch with her, but the Captain reckons I'm wasting my time. So I'm quitting from today. I've brought the copies of my daily reports. I don't reckon you'll find anything of interest, but you never know." He hauled from his pocket a fat envelope which he gave to Fenner.

"I'm planning to see the girl this morning," Fenner said. "She's my only link with Riley. I can't believe he left her flat. I have a hunch he must have told her something before he went underground."

"You're wasting your time," Doyle said. "We had her in and we questioned her for hours. Riley did walk out on her all right. The fact she's taken up with Eddie Schultz proves it. If she thought she had a chance of helping Riley spend the Blandish ransom money, she wouldn't have looked at Schultz."

"Well, I'm going to talk to her. I've got nothing else to work on."

"Watch your step," Doyle said. "Make sure Schultz isn't there when you call. That guy's dangerous."

"I'll watch it."

"I was in the Paradise Club last night," Doyle said. "I thought, before I quit watching the girl, I should see what her act was like. It's some act. I don't reckon she'll stay much longer with Schultz. She's got enough talent to hit Broadway."

"It beats me that a wild gang like the Grissons should have opened a club. Schulberg must have found a lot of dough all of a sudden."

"Yeah. I knew the club when Rocco ran it. You should see it now. You should see those hoods too: all got up in tuxedos, except Slim: he's the same as ever."

Fenner grimaced.

"There's a bad one if ever there was one."

"Yeah." Doyle grinned ruefully. "He nearly scared the life out of me last night. While the Borg girl was doing her act, I thought it might be an idea to get a closer look at the club. The opportunity came when they turned off the lights. I wanted to take a look upstairs. There was a hat check girl on guard, but I had a bit of luck. A couple of guys came in and checked their hats. One of them knocked over the bowl the girl keeps her tips in. The money fell behind the counter. She and the two guys were scrabbling for the money and I nipped up the stairs. There are seven rooms up there. Six of them bedrooms. The door at the end of the passage is fitted with a lock and a bolt outside which struck me as strange. Why a bolt outside? There was a TV set on. The door was locked from the inside. I didn't have long to look around when the Borg girl's act finished. I had just got to the head of the stairs when I heard a sound behind me. I looked around. The locked door was open. Slim Grisson was standing in the doorway. He had a knife in his hand. The sight of him certainly sent up my blood pressure. I didn't wait. I went down the stairs three at a time. The hat check girl looked at me as if I were a ghost. I kept going. When I got to the exit, I heard a shout. Schultz was coming after me. The bouncer at the door made a grab at me, but I socked him, got the door open and ran for my life. Schultz followed me as far as the main road, then he turned back."

"I'd like to have seen you on the run," Fenner said grinning. "Sounds like Ma Grisson's running a brothel up there. Did you tell Brennan?"

"Sure, but we can't do a thing. Nearly all the members are big shots with a load of influence. We'd never get a warrant to bust in there. Besides, the place is like a fort. The entrance door is made of steel and there are steel shutters covering the windows."

"Any idea what goes on in the locked room?"

"No. Your guess is as good as mine."

"Where will I find the Borg girl?"

"She and Schultz share an apartment at Malvern Court," Doyle said. "Top floor. But watch it. Don't walk in when Schultz's around."

When Doyle had gone, Fenner spent an hour reading through Doyle's reports. He didn't learn much except that Schultz always left the apartment at eleven o'clock to go to the club. Anna left at one o'clock to lunch at the club.

Fenner called Paula at the office.

"I'll be in after lunch," he said. "I'm going now to talk to the Borg girl. Any messages?"

"Mr. Blandish called. He's asking for news."

"I'll call him from here. Anything else?"

"A fat old party wants you to find her dog," Paula said, giggling. "I said you were allergic to dogs. That's right, isn't it?"

"Could be. Did she have any money?"

"Of course not." There was a pause, then Paula went on, "I wish you were allergic to strippers."

"Maybe I will be after I've talked to this one," Fenner said and hung up.

He called Blandish.

"I still think Anna Borg could tell us something," he said when Blandish came on the line. "Everything depends on how I approach her. The police have worked her over and got nothing out of her. I'm going to see if I can bribe her to talk. You said money is no object. Does that still go?"

"Of course," Blandish said. "What have you in mind?"

"I thought I'd tell her you would put her on Broadway if she can give us any information that will lead us to Riley. That might hook her."

"Try it," Blandish said.

"I'll call you back," and Fenner hung up.

5

Eddie Schultz came out of a heavy sleep with a start. The sun was shining through the blinds and he blinked, cursed, and then looked at the bedside clock. It was close on ten a.m.

Anna slept at his side. She was making a gentle snorting noise and Eddie scowled at her.

He got out of bed and searched for his cigarettes. He had a headache and he felt like hell. He lit a cigarette, then went into the sitting room. He poured himself a big whiskey and tossed it down.

The liquor exploded in his stomach. He groaned, then as the effects of the spirit reacted on his jaded system, he felt better. His sleep-sodden mind began to work.

He remembered the cop of last night. Ma had nearly flipped her lid when Slim had come down to say the cop had been upstairs. Eddie grimaced. Ma was right, of course. He had been careless, but it wasn't as if the cop had found out anything. Slim was the one who had made the real uproar. There had been a horrible moment when Eddie had been sure Slim was going to kill him. If it hadn't been for Ma, he was sure Slim would have stuck his goddamn knife into him. The memory of the scene brought Eddie out into a cold sweat.

Anyway, it was Ma's fault. If she had to be so stupid to let her nipple-headed son keep the Blandish girl, then she had to accept the responsibility if anything went wrong.

He returned to the bedroom.

Anna was awake. She had kicked off the bedclothes. She was lying flat on her back, staring up at the ceiling. She had on a sheer nylon nightgown.

"You're not doing your act now," Eddie growled on his way to the bathroom. "Cover up. You're indecent."

Ten minutes later, showered and shaved, he came into the bedroom. Anna still lay on the bed, still staring up at the ceiling.

"Instead of acting like a hypnotized fugitive from a honky-tonk," Eddie barked, "couldn't you get me some coffee?"

"Get it yourself; are you so helpless?" Anna sat up abruptly. "Eddie, I'm getting sick of this life. I've about had enough of it."

"Here we go again," Eddie said. "Two months ago you were hiding your talents behind a couple of moth-eaten fans for peanuts. I fix it for you to work in the best club in town. You get a hundred and fifty bucks a week and you're still not satisfied. What do you want? More money?"

"I want to get into big time," Anna said. She got off the bed and went into the bathroom.

Shrugging, Eddie went into the kitchen and made coffee. He took the coffee into the sitting room. Anna came in. She had put on a wrap and had fixed her hair. She saw the whiskey bottle that Eddie had forgotten to put back in the cabinet.

"Can't you lay off the booze for ten minutes?" she demanded. "What are you becoming—an alcoholic?"

"Oh, shut up!" Eddie snarled.

They drank their coffee in brooding silence.

"If I could find someone to finance me," Anna said suddenly, "I'd get out of this town."

"If I could find someone to finance me, I'd do the same," Eddie said sarcastically. "Will you stop yapping about your goddamn talent? Why don't you wake up? You're just a dime a dozen stripper. You're getting too big for your pants!"

Anna pushed aside her coffee cup.

"You men are all the same," she said wearily. "Frankie was the same. All you're interested in is my body and my looks. You aren't interested in me for myself."

Eddie groaned.

"If the candy tastes good, why worry what it's made of?"

"But suppose I was ugly, Eddie? Would you look at me? No, of course you wouldn't! But it would be me just the same."

"Oh, for the love of Mike! Can't we cut this out? I've got a hell of a headache. You're not ugly. So what?"

"I'm scared of getting old. I want to be in the bright lights before that happens. I want to be someone. I want to be a star: not a cheap stripper in a cheap club."

"Snap out of it, will you?" Eddie pleaded. "You're depressing me. You're doing all right. Can't you be content?"

"What's going on upstairs in the club?" Anna asked abruptly.

Eddie stiffened, looking sharply at her.

"Nothing. What do you mean?"

"Oh, yes there is. I'm not blind. I have an idea Slim's got a girl up there. Who is she, Eddie?"

"You're nuts!" Eddie said angrily. "Slim doesn't go for girls."

"I've seen Doc and Ma go up there. What's going on?"

"Nothing!" Eddie snapped. "So shut up!"

"I must have a hole in my head to have picked you to live with," Anna said angrily. "That's all I ever get from you—shut up!"

"You talk the crap you talk and that's all you can expect to hear." He went into the bedroom. It was time he left for the club. He dressed.

Anna came in.

"How much longer are you going to tag along with the Grisson gang?" she demanded. "How much longer are you going to lick that old bitch's boots?"

"And don't start that again," Eddie yelled, struggling into his coat. "I'm getting out of here. I've had all I want from you for one day."

Anna sneered.

"Small-time. What I ever saw in you! Run along, gigolo. Start your boot licking."

"Don't say you didn't ask for this," Eddie bellowed. "I've had enough of your big mouth. I'm going to teach you who's boss around here!

He pounced on her. Scooping her up, he slammed her face down across the bed. Holding her securely under the angle of his arm, he whisked up her clothes and began to spank her long and hard.

Kicking and struggling, Anna screamed like a train whistle. Eddie continued to slap her until his hand was burning and sore and the neighbors on either side of the apartment began hammering on the walls.

Then leaving her wriggling and screaming on the bed, Eddie left the apartment, slamming the door behind him.

Fenner, sitting in his car opposite the apartment block saw Eddie come out, his face dark with rage. He watched him get into the Buick and drive away.

Leaving his car, Fenner entered the apartment block and took the elevator to the top floor.

Before ringing the front door bell, Fenner checked to make sure his gun was ready for fast action, then he pushed the bell.

After a minute's wait, he rang again. The door remained unanswered. Fenner frowned. He was sure the girl was in. Why didn't she answer? He placed his thumb on the bell and kept it there.

After another two minutes, the door flew open. Her face contorted with pain and fury, her hair disheveled, Anna glared at him.

"What do you think this is—a fire station?" she screamed at him. "Get the hell out of here!" She attempted to slam the door, but Fenner had already wedged his foot against it.

"Miss Borg?"

"I'm not seeing anyone! Beat it!"

"But I am from Spewack, Anderson and Hart," Fenner lied. "Surely you want to see me?"

The name of the famous Broadway theatrical agents gave Anna pause. She stared at him.

"Are you kidding?" she demanded suspiciously.

"What should I want to kid you for?" Fenner asked blandly. "Spewack saw your act last night. He talked to Anderson, and if Hart had been on speaking terms with Anderson, you can bet your last nickel that Anderson would have talked to Hart. I have a proposition to discuss with you, Miss Borg."

"If this is a gag..." Anna began, then stopped. If it was true! she was thinking. Spewack, Anderson and Hart interested in *her!*

"If you don't want to discuss it that's okay with me," Fenner said, stepping back. "But let me tell you, baby, eight hundred strippers in this city would give their G-strings for the chance."

Anna hesitated no longer. She threw open the door.

"Well, come in..."

She led the way into the sitting room. She could kill Eddie, she was thinking. She had already inspected the damage he had inflicted on her. Suppose Spewack, Anderson and Hart wanted her for an audition? Suppose this guy wanted her to hop a taxi and go right downtown and do her act? How could she with the bruises she was carrying?

"Would you be interested to work in New York, Miss Borg?" Fenner asked, selecting the most comfortable chair and sitting down. "Or are you all tied up here?"

Anna's eyes opened wide.

"New York? Gee! I'd love it. No, I'm not tied up."

"You're not under contract with the Paradise Club?"

"It's only a week-to-week arrangement."

"That's fine. Sit down, Miss Borg: relax. I have a modern fairy story to tell you."

Absentmindedly, Anna sat down, but was up immediately with a gasp of pain.

"You sit on a tack or something?" Fenner asked, interested.

"Standing is good for my figure," Anna said, forcing a smile. "In my line, I have to watch, my figure."

"Relax, baby. I'll watch your figure. It'll be a pleasure."

"Now, see here, mister," Anna said, "If this turns out to be a gag..."

"This is no gag, Miss Borg," Fenner said smoothly. "We have a client with more money than sense. He wants to finance a musical on Broadway: that'll tell you how crazy he is, but who are we to discourage him? He's got the book, he's got the music and now he wants a star. He insists we use local talent. He made his money in Kansas City and he's sentimental. He wants some local girl to have the chance to be a star. We haven't found anyone yet as good as you. Do you want the chance?"

Anna's eyes opened wide.

"Do I *want* it? You really *mean* I'll be a *star* on Broadway?"

"There's only yourself to stop you. All Spewack has to do is to call our client, tell him about you and it'll be in the bag."

"Oh gee! It's too good to be true!"

"I said it was a modern fairy story, didn't I?" Fenner said airily. "A year's run on Broadway; then Hollywood. You have a great future ahead of you."

"When do I get a contract?" Anna asked, thinking she would pack at once and walk out on Eddie. "When do I meet Mr. Spewack or whoever it is?"

"I'll have a contract ready for you to sign this afternoon. You'll be lunching with Mr. Spewack in New York this time tomorrow."

"You're *sure* your client really wants me?" Anna asked, suddenly nervous. "Didn't you say Mr. Spewack had to telephone him first?"

"I'm glad you brought that up," Fenner said, lighting a cigarette. "There is that. Before we can talk to our client, there's a little situation that needs clearing up. We like you, Miss Borg, but frankly, we don't like your friends."

Anna stiffened.

"What do you mean?"

"Well, the boys you run around with aren't exactly the cream of society, are they? Take Eddie Schultz as an example. You'll have a lot of publicity, Miss Borg, once the news leaks out you're going to be the star of this show. We have to be careful it is favorable publicity."

Anna began to look worried.

"I'm not married to my friends. Once I get to Broadway, I wouldn't dream of associating with them any more."

"Well, that's nice to know, but a while back you were tied up with the notorious Frank Riley and he's right in the news. The press are certain to connect you with him. It could kill the whole show if that little item hit the headlines."

Anna suddenly felt sick with disappointment.

"I—I scarcely knew Riley," she said. "I—I just met him. You know how you meet people."

"Look, Miss Borg, you have to be frank with me. You don't meet people the way you met Riley just by chance. I've had to check on you. Don't imagine I like poking my nose into your affairs, but if we are going to make a big star out of you, we can't afford any scandal. I understand you knew Riley intimately."

Anna made a despairing gesture.

"Then why come here, raising my hopes? I knew this was a gag! I knew it was too good to be true."

"Hey, hey!" Fenner said. "Don't get depressed. There's always a way around every problem if one thinks hard enough. Now, look, Miss Borg, we can't hide up the fact that you have associated with hoodlums. That's impossible. So what do we do? We must use the fact to your advantage, and not to your disadvantage. They say the whole world loves a lover. I'll tell you who the world loves even better than a lover: a reformed character! That's what you're going to be. We're going to feed the press with a big sob story. We're going to tell them how you started from nothing; how you became infatuated with Riley without knowing he was a hoodlum; how you desperately tried to make him go straight when you finally found out what he was; how you lost faith in him when he kidnapped the Blandish girl. Do you get it? From the moment Riley walked out of your life, you have been trying to get away from your sordid environment, but Eddie Schultz appeared. He forced you to live with him. Then came this chance to appear on Broadway. You seized it with both hands. The hoods of Kansas City are now the thing of the past You're a reformed character."

Anna didn't think this sounded very convincing.

"Do you think *they'll* believe it?" she asked doubtfully.

"If they don't, baby, you're sunk," Fenner said, shaking his head.

Anna leaned against the mantel. She wished she could sit down. There was a hollow feeling inside her. She was sure now that this Broadway offer was going to be just a pipe dream.

"How are you going to make them believe it?" she asked. "Newspapermen! How I hate them! They spy and pry and they never leave you alone once they think they have a story. They don't give a damn how much they hurt you, how much mischief they cause, how many hearts they break so long as they get their story. I hate them all— the stinking sonsofbitches!"

It wouldn't do, Fenner thought, to tell her that he was once a newspaperman. She would probably shoot him.

"I'll tell you how we can convince them," he said. "Boy! What a story it would make! You'd be headline news throughout the country and good headlines at that."

"What are you talking about?" Anna snapped.

"Look, suppose through you, the Blandish girl was found. Imagine! Think what it would mean to you: television interviews, your picture in every newspaper, Blandish paying you a reward and your name on Broadway in four-foot lights!"

"Are you drunk?" Anna demanded, her face suddenly hard. "I don't know anything about the Blandish girl. What's the matter with you?"

"You knew Riley. For all you know, you may have the one clue that would lead the police to him."

Anna's eyes turned vicious.

"Yeah? Maybe Frankie did walk out on me, but I'd never give him away to the cops. What do you think I am? A squealer?"

Fenner shrugged his shoulders and got to his feet.

"If that's your idea of a reformed character, Miss Borg," he said. "I'm wasting my time. Well, it's been nice meeting you. I'll just have to tell Mr. Spewack he'll have to look elsewhere for our local talent."

"Wait a minute," Anna said hurriedly. "If I knew anything, I'd tell you, but I don't."

"When did you last see Riley?" Fenner asked.

"The morning before the snatch. Bailey telephoned him about the necklace. Riley told me he was going to grab it."

"Did he say anything about kidnapping the girl?"

"No."

"So you didn't hear anything from Riley after he left you on the morning of the kidnapping?"

Anna hesitated.

"Well, yes, I did. He telephoned me from Johnny Frisk's place."

Fenner drew in a long deep breath. Here it was at last! The new lead! Something she hadn't told the police.

"Johnny Frisk? You mean the old rummy who lives out at Lone Tree junction?"

"That's him." Anna suddenly stiffened. "How do you know

him?"

"I get around," Fenner said. "So Riley was out there? And you never told the police that?"

Anna was staring suspiciously at him.

"Just who are you?" she said. "This is a gag, isn't it? Are you a cop?"

A sound made both of them look towards the door. Someone had unlocked the front door. Quick steps sounded, then the door leading into the sitting room jerked open.

Eddie Schultz came in.

"I forgot my goddamn wallet..." he began then he saw Fenner.

"Pardon me, pal," Fenner said quietly and uncorked a right hook that hit Eddie flush on his jaw. Eddie went down as if he was pole-axed.

Anna turned and rushed into the bedroom, but by the time she had got her gun, Fenner had vanished.

Slowly Eddie sat up, holding his jaw. He stared at Anna. Then he got to his feet.

"What's going on?" he demanded shakily. "Hell! That punk's nearly bust my jaw! What was a goddamn newspaperman doing in here?"

Anna stared at him in horror.

"A newspaperman?" she screamed.

Her expression sent a chill up Eddie's spine. He had a terrible premonition that his future was about to explode in his face.

6

Ma Grisson was just finishing an early lunch from a well-loaded tray on her desk when the telephone rang.

Doc Williams who was keeping her company, drinking, but not eating, picked up the receiver.

"It's Eddie." Eddie Schultz's voice sounded strained. "Ma there?"

Doc offered the receiver to Ma.

"Eddie."

She took the receiver, wiping her mouth with the back of her hand.

"What is it?"

"Trouble, Ma. Remember Dave Fenner who worked on the *Tribune*? He's been here while I was out. He kidded Anna he could put her on Broadway if she could give him a line on the Blandish snatch. She told him the last time she had spoken to Riley was at Johnny's place. He's gone off like a bat out of hell."

"What?" Ma bellowed, her raddled face turning purple. "I know that sonofabitch! He'll hammer the truth out of Johnny! I always said we should have knocked that old drunk off!"

"That's why I phoned, Ma." Eddie sounded badly shaken. "Listen, Ma, we can't blame Anna. She didn't know what we know."

"Come down here!" Ma snarled.

"The punk's nearly bust my jaw," Eddie said. "I'm feeling like hell. I thought you'd better get Flynn..."

"Don't tell me what to do!" Ma snarled and slammed down the receiver.

Doc's face had gone grey. He looked helplessly at Ma.

"Don't sit there like a damned old dummy!" Ma bawled at him. "Get Flynn, Woppy and Slim! Hurry!"

Doc hurried out.

Within a few minutes Flynn and Woppy came in. They both looked startled. Doc came in a moment later with Slim who was scratching his head and yawning.

"Listen," Ma said, "we could be in trouble. That chippy of Eddie's told a newspaperman about Johnny. This guy has probably gone out to talk to Johnny. If he gets tough with the old drunk, Johnny will talk. You three go out there fast. Wipe Johnny out. We should have done it before now. If the newspaperman's there when you arrive, knock him off too. Bury them both. Get going!"

"It's a four hour drive," Flynn grumbled. "You sure..."

"You heard what I said!" Ma roared, jumping up and smashing her big fists on the desk. "And drive like hell! You've got to get there before Fenner does!"

Slim said, "I'm not going. To hell with it! I've got something better to do."

Ma came around the desk. She looked so mad even Slim drew back.

"You're going! You're getting too goddamn soft! If you don't shut that old drunk's mouth, you'll lose your plaything. You hear me? Now get the hell out of here!"

Muttering, Slim followed Flynn and Woppy out of the room.

"As bad as that, Ma?" Doc said feebly. He wished he hadn't had that extra drink. He was feeling dizzy.

"Women! Women! Women!" Ma snarled, pounding on the desk. "Always the same! Barker... Karpis... Dillinger... they all went the same way... because of women! Everything I've planned could be shot... just because a goddamn chippy opens her goddamn mouth!"

As Woppy and Slim made for the exit, Flynn who had made a date with Maisey for the evening, paused by her as she was arranging her cloakroom counter.

"We got business, babe," he said. "The date's off. I'll be lucky if I get back by nine."

He ran on down and joined Woppy and Slim as they bundled into the Dodge.

Maisey shrugged. She wasn't sorry the date was broken. Flynn was mean to go out with. He just wouldn't keep his hands to himself.

She put on her coat. It was time for lunch and she was hungry. She nodded to MacGowan, the bouncer, as she went down the stairs.

"See you around nine, Mac," she said. "I'm going to nourish my curves."

MacGowan grinned. He watched her hips swing down the stairs into the courtyard.

Maisey always went to the same place for lunch. It sold the best hamburgers in town and it wasn't far from the club.

Rocco knew this, and happening to be near the restaurant he decided to eat there himself. Maybe, if he talked right, he might get some information from the doll. She looked dumb enough, but maybe she might let drop something he could use against Ma.

On his way to the restaurant, he had spotted the Dodge edging its way through the heavy traffic and he was surprised to see Slim as well as Woppy and Flynn in the car. He wondered where they were going.

He found Maisey sitting at a corner table, carefully studying the menu.

"Hello, beautiful," he said. "Mind if I buy you a lunch?"

Maisey looked up and smiled. She knew Rocco had once owned the Paradise Club. She was flattered he should pay her any attention.

"I won't fight against it," she said. "I'm always glad of company."

Rocco pulled out a chair and sat down. His legs ached and his feet were sore. He had had a hard morning but at least now he was finished for the day.

He ordered the lunch special and a crab salad for Maisey.

"Well, baby, how's the club going?" he asked. "Doing all right?"

"Sure," Maisey said. "I guess they must be coining money." She sighed. "I wish some of it came my way. I only get a lousy thirty bucks and tips and I have to provide my own uniform."

"I should have thought you'd have got more than that. With the shape you have on, you could do better in a honky-tonk."

Maisey looked indignant.

"I wouldn't be seen dead in one of those joints. I'll have you know I'm not that kind of a girl."

"Pardon me, my mistake," Rocco said.

The food came and for a while they ate in silence. From time to time Rocco glanced at the girl, trying to make up his mind how to proposition her. He decided regretfully the only thing she could be interested in was money.

When Maisey had finished, she sat back with a sigh of content.

"That was pretty nice. Thanks: you're nice."

"I'm not so lousy," Rocco said modestly. "Say, baby, how would you like to make yourself thirty bucks?"

Maisey looked suspiciously at him.

"Doing what?"

He patted her hand.

"Not what you're thinking. It's strictly business. How's about you coming back to my apartment and discussing it with me?"

"No, thank you," Maisey said firmly. "I've heard that one before."

Rocco pretended to be shocked.

"You've got me wrong, baby. I have an idea I want to talk

over with you: an idea that could earn you another thirty bucks a week. But if it doesn't interest you..."

"Another thirty bucks a week?" Maisey sat up. "What's wrong with talking about it right here and now?"

Rocco shook his head. He got to his feet.

"It's strictly confidential, but forget it. I'll find another baby who isn't so fussy as you." He signaled for the check and paid from a big roll of bills which he let Maisey see. He put the roll back in his pocket, aware that Maisey was eyeing it greedily. "Well, thanks for your company. Be seeing you."

"Hey! Don't be in such a rush. Maybe I could change my mind. Where's your apartment anyway?"

"Just around the corner. Take us two minutes."

Maisey hesitated, then she got to her feet.

"The risks we poor girls have to run for a little dough," she said. "Well, okay, but remember—no funny business."

"The idea never entered my head," Rocco lied.

He had a convenient little apartment on the third floor above a filling and garage station with a back entrance though a courtyard that was used as a parking lot.

Maisey was surprised to see how nicely the big sitting room-bedroom was arranged and kept. The furniture was of light oak. A few rugs made islands on the polished floor. The chairs were big and overstuffed. There was a vast divan capable of sleeping four people: five at a pinch.

Maisey stood gaping at the divan.

"That's pretty ambitious for a little guy like you, isn't it?" she asked as he helped her off with her coat. "I'd have thought you would have got lost in that desert."

"You'd be surprised what goes on in that bed," Rocco said with a wink. "Me—I like plenty of room to maneuver in."

"I'll say you do," Maisey said admiringly and giggled.

As she began to wander around the room, peering at his possessions, Rocco fixed two stiff drinks.

"Come and sit down, baby," he said, "I want to talk business to you."

Maisey lowered herself into one of the big lounging chairs. It was so deep, her knees were higher than her head. As Rocco handed her the highball, he looked with interest at what he could see of her from where he was standing.

"Talk away," Maisey said. "I'm listening."

Rocco waved his glass at her. Maisey drank half the whiskey in her glass, then blew out her cheeks.

"Say, this is strong enough to knock over a pregnant mule."

"You think so?" Rocco said and patted her exposed knee. "But then you're no pregnant mule."

Maisey giggled. She didn't often get a chance to drink good Scotch. As Rocco offered her a cigarette, she emptied her glass.

"I'll give you a refill," Rocco said, taking her glass to the cabinet.

"Only a small one," Maisey said, settling herself comfortably, "or I'll get cockeyed."

"Why should you worry?" Rocco said as he sloshed four inches of whiskey into the glass and a little soda. He put the glass within her reach, then he sat opposite her.

"I'm looking for a smart girl who can get me some information. This is strictly confidential, baby. I want to get a line on the Grisson gang. You're on the inside. You could get me what I want."

Maisey didn't like this idea at all. She was scared of Ma Grisson. Monkeying with Ma could be dangerous. She drank some of the whiskey while she attempted to think. To Maisey any form of thinking came hard. Rocco could almost hear her brain creak.

"If the idea doesn't jell, baby," he said, "forget it. I'll play you some records instead. I've got a great library of jazz, but if you want to pick up a steady thirty bucks a week, here's your chance."

"What sort of information do you want?" Maisey asked cautiously.

"I'm not fussy," Rocco said. "I haven't been in the joint since Ma took over. Anything illegal going on in there?"

Maisey belched gently.

"Plenty," she said. "I get the jitters sometimes in case there's a raid."

"Don't be coy," Rocco said, "Let's have some details."

Maisey wagged her finger at him.

"Let's have some money first, bright boy."

Rocco sighed. Women seemed, these days, he thought, to think only of money. He took out his roll, thumbed off twenty one dollar bills and handed them to Maisey.

"I trust you, sweetheart," he said, wondering if he was wasting his money. "Now give me something."

Maisey finished her drink. She was feeling a little dizzy.

"Let's see." She frowned up at the ceiling. "They've got a roulette table. That's illegal, isn't it? Then upstairs they have a brothel. That's illegal too. I'll tell you something else. All the doors are made of steel and there are steel shutters to the windows. By the time the cops break in, I'll bet there'll be nothing to see."

Rocco looked at her unhappily. He knew most of what she had told him. He tried another angle.

"Where were the boys going just now?" he asked. "I saw Flynn, Woppy and Slim in the Dodge heading out of town."

Maisey crossed one long leg over the other. Rocco blinked. From where he sat, he could see plenty.

"I wouldn't know," she said. "Flynn said it was business."

She blew out her cheeks. "Phew! that Scotch is strong! He said they wouldn't be back until nine. How's about another drink?"

Patiently, Rocco fixed her another drink.

"Keep trying," he said. "Is there anything out-of-the-way going on in the club? Anything odd?"

Maisey groped for her drink and nearly dropped it.

"Whoops! That nearly lost good liquor," she said. "I think I'm just a little bit plastered."

"Not you," Rocco said, helping her put the drink on the table. "You're just happy."

"Yeah, maybe." She tried to focus him without success. "I'll tell you something: Slim's got a girl friend."

Rocco shook his head.

"No, baby, not Slim. He's never had a girl friend, and never will have. He's not built that way. Try something else."

Maisey glared aggressively at him.

"Are you calling me a liar? I'm telling you he's got a girl who he keeps locked in a room upstairs."

Rocco felt a sudden quickening of excitement. Could he be getting somewhere with this dumb chick?

"Why does he keep her locked up?" he asked.

Maisey fanned herself with her hand, shaking her head.

"Search me. Mind you, if that streak of horror took a notion for me, I'd have to be locked up if he was to get anywhere with me." She giggled. "I'm sorry for her. Slim scarcely ever leaves her. He stays in that locked room with her nearly all the time."

Rocco was getting intrigued.

"Have you ever seen her?"

"Just once, but I hear, every night before the club opens, Slim takes her for a walk. They don't stay out long. I reckon he just walks her around the block and brings her back. I got to the club a little early: my watch was wrong. That's when I saw her. Slim and the girl were coming down the stairs. I only got a glimpse of her because Ma appeared and hustled me into the Ladies' room."

"What was the girl like?" Rocco asked, listening intently.

"I didn't see her face. She had a scarf over her head and pulled across her face, but there was something queer about her. She walked down the stairs as if she couldn't see —the way blind people walk."

"Ma know about all this?"

"Sure, and Doc too. Doc goes up to her room every day."

Rocco thought for a moment. This might be worth investigating, he thought.

"I want to see this girl," he said. "How do I do it?"

Maisey smiled drunkenly at him.

"I'm not stopping you. Stick around the club between ten and eleven and you'll see Slim and her taking a walk."

If Slim was going to be out of town until nine, Rocco thought, there wouldn't be much chance of seeing this mysterious girl tonight.

"You don't tell me he takes her out through the front entrance?" he said.

Maisey was suddenly feeling faint. The room was moving slowly up and down with the motion of a ship.

"There's a back entrance," she said, "through the warehouse next door."

Rocco smiled. He was now sure he hadn't wasted his money.

"That Scotch seems to have been a little too much for you, baby," he said. "Come and lie down."

"You've got something there," Maisey said. "I feel terrible."

Rocco pulled her out of the chair. She staggered against him and would have fallen if he hadn't caught hold of her.

"Whoops! Someone is rocking my dream boat," she said and clung hard to him.

Rocco looked at the clock on the mantel. The time was a little after three. He guided Maisey to the divan and lowered her gently onto its wide softness.

"The same old, old story," she said, her eyes closed. "The guy says strictly business and it's always strictly something else."

Rocco lowered the blinds.

He believed in the right atmosphere.

Maisey sighed happily when he took her in his arms.

CHAPTER FOUR

1

Fenner arrived at the foot of the dirt road leading to Johnny's shack soon after four o'clock in the afternoon. He had driven hard and fast, and he was sharply conscious of the possibility that some of the Grisson gang could be coming after him.

Before leaving town, he had paused long enough to telephone Paula, telling her where he was going.

"I think I'm on to something," he said. "Call Brennan and tell him what's cooking. Tell him to come to Johnny's place fast."

"Why don't you wait for him?" Paula asked anxiously. "Why go out there alone?"

"Quit worrying," Fenner said. "Tell Brennan," and he hung up.

But now, as he drove his car off the road and behind a thicket, he began to think Paula's suggestion had been a sensible one. This place was miles from anywhere: it was lonelier than a pauper's grave.

He got out of the car, satisfied himself it couldn't be seen from the road, then he started up the dirt road towards Johnny's shack.

Half-way up the road, he paused to pull his gun and slide off the safety catch. He was pretty sure none of the Grisson gang had got ahead of him, but he wasn't taking any chances.

The evening sun was hot, and Fenner, who hated walking, cursed under his breath as he left the dirt road and started along the twisting path that led directly to the shack.

Two hundred yards ahead of him, he could see the dense wood through which he was walking open out onto a clearing. He slowed, picking his way silently, his eyes and ears alert.

A blue-winged jay suddenly flew out of a tree close by with a flapping of wings that startled Fenner. He looked up, his heart skipping a beat and then he grinned.

I'm as jittery as an old maid with a man under her bed, he

told himself, and moved on cautiously to the edge of the clearing. He paused behind a tree and looked at the shabby wooden shack that stood in the center of the clearing.

It looked as if Johnny was at home. The door stood open and wood smoke curled lazily from the single chimney.

Keeping his gun hand down by his side and out of sight, Fenner walked silently over the rough grass until he reached the front door. He paused just outside the shack to listen.

He could hear Johnny humming to himself. He moved forward and paused in the open doorway.

Johnny, his back turned, was bending over the stove. He was cooking bacon in a frying pan. The smell of the bacon made Fenner's nose twitch.

Fenner looked quickly around the large dirty room. The gun rack, holding two shotguns was by the door, well away from Johnny.

He stepped into the room, covering the old man with his gun.

"Hello, Johnny," he said softly.

Johnny stiffened, then shuddered. He straightened and turned very slowly. His red, raddled face went slack with fright at the sight of Fenner. His dim, watery eyes opened wide at the sight of the gun in Fenner's hand.

"Take it easy," Fenner said. "Remember me, Johnny?"

The old man seemed to be having trouble with his breathing.

"What are you pointing that gun at me for?" he croaked.

Fenner lowered the gun.

"Remember me?" he repeated.

Johnny blinked at him, frowning.

"You're the guy from the newspaper, aren't you?"

"That's right," Fenner said. "Sit down, Johnny, I want to talk to you."

Johnny lowered himself onto an upturned box. He seemed glad to get the weight off his legs. He shoved the frying pan off the direct heat of the stove and then with a shaking hand, he rubbed his bristly chin while he squinted up at Fenner.

"Now listen, Johnny," Fenner said, "you could be in bad trouble. You could go to jail for a long stretch. You wouldn't like that, would you? No booze; no nothing. You come clean with me and I'll cover you. All I want from you is some information."

"I don't know nothing about nothing," Johnny said. "I don't want you around here. I just want to be left alone."

"Riley and his mob were here about three months ago, weren't they?" Fenner asked.

Johnny stiffened. He looked wildly around the room as if seeking a way of escape.

"I don't know nothing about Riley."

"Listen, you old fool," Fenner said sharply, "lying won't get you anywhere. They had the Blandish girl with them. Riley called his girl friend from here. She's talking. So far, she has only talked to me, but if she starts talking to the cops, you'll be in trouble. They'll work you over, Johnny, until you do open your mouth. Now come on. Riley was here, wasn't he?"

Johnny hesitated, then with a cunning expression in his eyes, he nodded.

"Yeah, that's right. He and Bailey and Old Sam and a girl. They didn't stay long; not more than ten minutes. I wouldn't have them here. They were too hot. I wasn't taking a chance of getting in bad with the cops so I told them to keep moving. Riley called his girl, then they got back into their car and beat it. I don't know where they went."

But the way he told it, the way he looked convinced Fenner he was lying.

"Okay, Johnny," he said mildly. "That puts you right in the clear. Just too bad you don't know where they went Blandish is offering a reward for information. Wouldn't you like to lay your hands on fifteen thousand bucks?"

Johnny blinked. It was now over three months since he had buried Riley, Bailey and Old Sam, and what a job that had been! Schultz had promised him a cut of the ransom money, but he hadn't had it. He knew the ransom had been paid. He had taken the trouble to go into town and buy a newspaper. He had been double-crossed and he felt mean and bitter about it.

"Fifteen thousand bucks?" he repeated. "How do I know I would get it?"

"I'd see you got it, Johnny," Fenner said.

Better not, Johnny told himself. It was too dangerous to monkey with the Grisson gang.

He shook his head reluctantly.

"I don't know nothing," he said.

"You're lying," Fenner said and moved over to the old man. "Do you want me to work you over, Johnny? Like this?" He hit Johnny a backhand slap across his face: not a hard blow, but hard enough to make the old man rock and nearly fall off the box. "Come on! Spill it!" Fenner went on, raising his voice. "Where's Riley? You can either pick up fifteen thousand bucks or take a beating! What's it to be?"

Johnny cringed away.

"I don't know nothing," he said desperately. "If you want to know anything ask the Grisson gang. They were right here. They fixed Riley..." He stopped, his raddled face turning grey.

"The Grisson gang?" Fenner stiffened to attention. "How did they fix Riley?"

But Johnny was staring past Fenner through the open door. His expression of terror chilled Fenner's blood.

Fenner looked over his shoulder. He saw a shadow fall across the open doorway: the shadow of a man with a Thompson gun in his hands.

Then everything seemed to happen at once.

Fenner dived to the floor, well clear of Johnny. He rolled towards a big iron tank that stood across a corner of the room: a tank in which Johnny used to store his horse feed when he owned a horse. As he jerked himself behind the tank with one swift movement, there came the violent and continuous sound of the Thompson firing.

A stream of lead ripped into Johnny's chest. The old man was thrown over backwards. He rolled over, twitching, then his body went limp. Seconds later, Fenner was nearly deafened as slugs hammered against the side of the tank. He crouched down, his heart thumping, his breath whistling through his clenched teeth.

For three or four seconds the slugs beat against the side of the iron tank, making a noise like a giant rivet-gun at work. Then the shooting stopped. The sudden silence was nearly as violent as the gun fire had been.

Fenner wiped his sweating face with the back of his hand. He guessed the Grisson gang had arrived. He was in a hell of a jam. He knew if he attempted to look around the side of the tank, he would have his head blown off. His one hope was that

Brennan would be arriving soon, but would he arrive in time?

He flattened himself in the dust and put his ear to the wooden floor. He couldn't hear anything. He doubted if any of the gang out there would have the nerve to come in and tackle him.

Then he heard the murmur of men's voices. There was a pause, then a man shouted, "Come on out! We know you're in there. Come out with your hands in the air!"

Fenner grinned crookedly. Not likely, he told himself, if you want me, come and get me. He waited.

The Thompson started up again. The noise made Fenner wince. He could hear some of the slugs dropping into the tank, having cut their way through the outer side of the tank. The gun stopped firing.

"Come on out, punk!" a voice bawled.

He lay motionless and silent.

He heard a man say, "Give it to me! Get down flat, both of you."

Fenner stiffened. He knew what was coming. They were going to blast him out with a pineapple. He flattened down, protecting his head with his arms. The few seconds' pause of silence seemed an eternity. Then he heard something drop on the floor. The bomb went off with a devastating bang. The blast lifted him and tossed him against the side of the tank.

He rolled over onto his back, choking and gasping. For a moment, everything became very clear and sharply etched. He could see the roof of the shack above him. It was sagging. As he watched, there came the sound of splintering wood, then the roof came crashing down on top of him.

Something hit him a violent blow on the side of his head. Bright lights flashed before his eyes, then he felt himself falling into a black, bottomless pit.

2

The darkness was suddenly pierced by a hot, hard light. Fenner heard himself groan as he raised his hand to shield his eyes.

"You're okay," a distant voice said. "Come on; come on. Don't just lie there pitying yourself."

Fenner made the effort. He opened his eyes and shook his head. He became aware of a man bending over him. The man's face swam into focus. He recognized Brennan, and he slowly sat up.

"That's the idea." Brennan said. "You're okay. What's all the fuss about?"

Fenner nursed his head in his hands.

"Who's making a fuss?" he demanded, and then grunted as his head began to ache violently. Hands took bold of him and hoisted him to his feet. "Don't rush me!" he went on, leaning on the arm of a policeman. "Hell! My head feels as if it has been kicked by a horse."

"No horse around here," Brennan said cheerfully. "What happened?"

Fenner drew in a deep breath. He felt stronger now. Gently he ran his fingers through his hair and winced, but finding he hadn't a hole in his head, he managed to grin wryly.

"Seen anyone around?" he asked.

"Just you and what's left of Johnny," Brennan said. "Who let off the pineapple?"

"Johnny dead?"

"Sure is—deader than a mackerel."

Fenner turned and looked at the wrecked shack. He was feeling better every minute. With a slightly unsteady step, he moved out of the sun and sat down on an uprooted tree. He took out a pack of cigarettes and lit one while the three policemen and Brennan stood watching him impatiently.

Fenner wasn't to be hurried. His mind was at work. He suddenly snapped his fingers and pointed to Brennan.

"Know something?" he said. "We're going to bust the Blandish snatch! Here's what you do! Get your men to look around. They'll be looking for ground recently dug. Hurry it up!"

"What's the idea?" Brennan demanded.

"Someone's been buried here recently. Come on, get going! You want to bust this thing, don't you?"

Brennan gave orders and the three policemen went off in different directions. Brennan came to sit by Fenner's side.

"Who's been buried?" he asked. "Let's have it, dick, don't act mysterious."

"It's my bet Riley, Bailey and Old Sam are buried around

here," Fenner said. "I could be wrong, but I don't think I am."

Brennan gaped at him.

"Who threw the pineapple?"

"Again I wouldn't know, but I'm willing to bet it was one of the Grisson gang."

"What would they want to do that to you for?"

"Leave it lie for a moment, Brennan," Fenner said. "One step at a time."

Brennan scowled at him, then he lit a cigarette and stared across the clearing at the ruined shack.

"You were lucky to get out of that alive," he said. "I thought you were done for."

"That makes two of us," Fenner said.

A small bird suddenly swooped out of a tree and hopped from twig to twig on a nearby bush. Fenner watched it without interest. He was sweating and his mouth was dry. He was thinking of the thirty thousand dollars Blandish had promised him if he cracked the case.

A sudden shout made both men turn sharply.

"Sounds like someone's found something," Fenner said getting stiffly to his feet.

Both men walked towards the sound of shouting, forcing their way through the thick shrubs. It didn't take them long to catch up with the other two policemen. They all entered a small clearing where the third policeman was pointing to the ground. The soil had obviously been disturbed although it had been covered with leaves and dead branches.

"This is where someone starts digging," Fenner said and sat down in the shade.

Brennan gave orders. Two of the policemen hurried off. After a while they returned with a couple of spades they had found in Johnny's outhouse. They peeled off their tunics and began to dig.

It was hot work and they were sweating before they found what they were looking for. Suddenly they stopped digging. One of the men knelt on the grass and reached into the shallow hole. Fenner got to his feet and walked over to watch. The policeman was scraping the soil away with his band. A faint smell of death came from the hole that made Fenner grimace. Suddenly he saw a mud-matted head coming to light. He stepped back.

"A dead man here, Captain," the policeman said, looking up at Brennan.

"There'll be three," Fenner said. "Let's get out of here, Brennan. Let's get back to headquarters. This is urgent now."

Brennan told the three policemen he would send out a truck and the Medical Officer. He and Fenner went down to Fenner's car.

"The writing went up on the wall when Ma Grisson took over the Paradise Club," Fenner said as he got into the car, waving Brennan to the driving seat. "We should have guessed how she financed that deal. She bought the club with the Blandish ransom money!" Brennan paused as he was about to start the car.

"How the hell do you figure that one out?" he demanded.

"It's not so hard to figure. Ma gave out that Schulberg gave her the money. Schulberg deals in hot money. He has probably cleaned up with the ransom. Johnny told me just before he was knocked off that Grisson and his gang were with Riley at Johnny's place. Somehow Grisson must have found out that Riley had snatched the Blandish girl. He would know the only place Riley could take her would be to Johnny's. He and his gang went there, knocked Riley and the other two off and took the girl. Blandish paid the ransom to Grisson, thinking he was Riley. It adds up. As soon as the ransom was paid, Ma Grisson opens the Paradise Club. What a sweet setup for them! Riley gets the blame and they are sitting pretty."

"Where's the proof?" Brennan asked. "Even if my boys do dig up Riley and the other two, it still doesn't mean Grisson killed them. With Johnny dead, we haven't any proof."

Fenner nodded.

"That's right. We'll have to find proof. Let's not go off half-cocked on this. Know what I think?"

"What do you think, superman?" Brennan asked sarcastically. He was pushing the car hard and they were roaring down the long main road.

"I think the Blandish girl is in the Paradise Club," Fenner said. As Brennan turned to stare at him, Fenner yelled, "Look where you're driving!"

Brennan slammed on his brakes and drew up by the side of the road.

"What are you getting at?"

"Remember Doyle said there was a room upstairs in the club kept locked. It's my bet she's in there!"

"We'll soon find out," Brennan said, starting the car again.

"Will we?" Fenner said thoughtfully. "The club is like a fort. It'll take time to bust in. By the time we do get in the girl will either be dead or removed. Blandish wants her alive. If we're going to bring her out alive, we'll have to handle this with kid gloves. We've got to use our heads, Brennan."

"Okay, so we use our heads," Brennan said. "Where will that get us?"

"I don't know," Fenner said and lit a cigarette. "Let me think about it."

For the next half hour Brennan continued to drive fast while Fenner coped with his aching head and his thoughts. As Brennan slowed down before entering a small farming town, Fenner said, "We'll pick up Anna Borg. She knows that Grisson and Riley met at Johnny's. She's our only witness. We don't want her knocked off. Besides being our only witness, she spends a lot of time in the club. Maybe she knows the Blandish girl is there. Maybe she doesn't know the Grisson gang wiped out Riley. If we tell her, there's a chance she might rat on them."

Brennan pulled up outside a drug store.

"I'll get things going," he said.

Fenner watched him enter a phone booth. He looked at his watch. The time was a little after six p.m. They were still three hours' driving distance from Kansas City.

He wondered if the Blandish girl really was in the club. If she was, she had been in the hands of the gang for over three months.

He grimaced.

What had happened to her during that time? He thought of Slim Grisson and he shook his head.

Brennan came out and got into the car.

"I've given orders for Anna Borg to be picked up. A couple of the boys will be watching the club."

Fenner grunted.

"Let's go," he said.

Brennan started the car and drove fast out of the town and onto the highway.

3

A little after five o'clock, Rocco left his apartment and walked briskly to the main street. He had rested on his vast bed for an hour after Maisey had gone.

The mysterious girl Maisey had told him about intrigued him. He had decided he would investigate. He knew Slim, Flynn and Woppy wouldn't be back until after nine. At this hour, it was unlikely Eddie Schultz would be in the club. That left only Ma Grisson and Doc Williams to worry about. He would have to be careful, but he felt pretty sure he could handle Doc if he had to. Ma scared him, but with any luck he wouldn't run into her.

It was Saturday, and the warehouse next to the club was closed. Maisey had told him there was an entrance to the club through the warehouse. This entrance he intended to find.

The building next to the warehouse was a shabby hotel. He knew the owner, a fat Greek whose name was Nick Papolos. He told Nick with a wink that he wanted to admire the view from the hotel roof. Nick stared at him, shrugged his fat shoulders and told him to help himself.

"Just don't get me into no trouble," the Greek said.

Rocco patted his arm.

"You know me, Nick," he said. "Strictly no trouble."

He took the elevator to the top floor, opened a skylight and got onto the flat roof. From there it was easy to enter the warehouse. It took him twenty minutes of careful searching before he found the hidden door leading into the club. It took him only a few seconds to pick the lock and get the door open. He stepped into a dark passage, gun in hand, his heart thumping. At the end of the passage was another locked door. This he opened without difficulty, then he found himself looking into a large, well-furnished room with a big television set facing him. Across the room was a door, and for a long moment, he stood hesitating. He moved silently to the door and listened against the panel. Hearing nothing, he opened the door and peered into the ornate bedroom.

Miss Blandish was sitting on the edge of the bed, staring with blank eyes at the floor. She had on a white cotton dress that Slim had bought her. A cigarette burned between her slim white fingers.

Rocco stared at her. He had never seen a more beautiful girl. There was something familiar about her face. He felt almost sure he had seen this girl somewhere before.

He moved silently into the room.

Miss Blandish didn't look up. She suddenly let the cigarette slip out of her fingers. It fell on the carpet and listlessly, she put her foot on it.

"Hello," Rocco said softly. "What are you doing here?"

The heavy drugged eyes stared at him.

"Please go away," she said.

Her pinpoint pupils told Rocco plenty.

"What's your name, baby?" he asked.

"My name?" She frowned. "I don't know. Please go away. He wouldn't like you to be here."

Where had he seen this girl before? Rocco asked himself. He looked at the red-gold hair. Then a surge of excitement ran through him. In his mind, he saw the dozens of pictures that had appeared in all the newspapers of this girl. This redhead, sitting so lifelessly on the bed, was John Blandish's daughter! How the hell had Grisson got hold of her? He was so excited he could scarcely breathe. What a chance to level his score! Besides, there was a reward of fifteen thousand dollars for this girl!

"Your name's Blandish, isn't it?" he said, trying to control his shaking voice. "You were kidnapped nearly four months ago. Don't you remember?"

She peered at him.

"Blandish?" she repeated. "That's not my name."

"Yes, it is," Rocco said. "You'll remember in a little while. Come on, baby, you and me are going for a walk."

"I don't know who you are. Please go away."

Rocco put his hand on her arm, but she jerked back, her face tightening with fear.

"Don't touch me!"

The shrill tone of her voice brought Rocco out in a sweat. Any moment Doc Williams or Ma Grisson could walk in. He was determined to get the girl to his place. He was tempted to knock her unconscious and carry her out, but he knew this would be impossible in broad daylight.

"Come on," he said, his voice hardening. "Slim's waiting for you. I've got to take you to him."

This was an inspired idea. Miss Blandish immediately got to her feet. She allowed Rocco to lead her into the sitting room. He guided her through the door to the passage leading to the warehouse. She moved like a zombie.

It wasn't until he had got her from the warehouse, down the alley that ran along the back of the club and the warehouse and into a cruising taxi that he began to relax. He told the driver who was staring curiously at Miss Blandish to take them to his apartment.

While this was going on, Ma Grisson was talking to Flynn on the telephone.

"It's all fixed," Flynn was saying. "We're on our way back. No trouble at all."

"Both of them?" Ma asked.

"Yeah."

"Fine, fine. Hurry on back," and Ma hung up. Her office door opened and Eddie Schultz came in. He had a livid bruise on the side of his jaw.

Ma glared at him.

"You and your goddamn women!" she snarled. "That chippy could have blown the lid right off this setup."

Eddie sat down. He lit a cigarette and fingered his jaw.

"It wasn't Anna's fault. What's happened?"

"It's fixed, thanks to me. Flynn's just been on. They wiped out both Johnny and that punk, Fenner."

"It wasn't Anna's fault," Eddie said. "All she told this guy..."

"I'm not having her in the club again," Ma said. "I'm not having anyone here who talks."

Eddie started to say something, then seeing the evil look in Ma's eyes, he stopped. He remembered Anna had asked who the girl had been in Slim's room. If he told Anna Ma wouldn't have her in the club, Anna might turn nasty. She might even start talking about this girl. He knew if he told Ma this, she would get Flynn to knock Anna off.

Ma saw by his expression that he was uneasy and worried about something.

"What's on your mind?" she asked, staring at him.

"Look, Ma," Eddie said, "so far we have got away with murder. We have this club: we have all the money in the world and we're sitting pretty. But for how long? Okay, Anna talked and it looked like the setup was going to blow up in our faces. We had to knock off Johnny and this newspaper guy. So we're now sitting pretty again, but for how long, Ma?"

Ma moved restlessly. She knew what Eddie was driving at. There came a tap on the door and Doc Williams came in! His face was flushed. Ma could see he had been drinking again.

"What happened?" he asked as he sat down near Ma.

"It's all fixed," Ma said. "You've got nothing to worry about."

"Until the next time," Eddie said. "Why don't you get smart, Ma? So long as the girl is here, we're sitting on dynamite."

"Are you telling me what to do?" Ma snarled, glaring at him.

"That's what I'm trying to do," Eddie said. "We would be in the clear with not a thing to worry about if it wasn't for the Blandish girl. Why did we have to knock Johnny off? Because we were scared the cops would bust in here and find the girl. If she wasn't here, we could have let the cops in and we could have laughed at them."

Doc took out a handkerchief and wiped his sweating face.

"He's right, Ma," he said. "So long as she's here we're vulnerable."

Ma got to her feet and began to pace up and down while Eddie and Doc watched her.

"Couldn't she have a heart attack?" Eddie asked Doc. "Slim wouldn't know you had anything to do with it." He was putting his finger right on the problem. He knew both Ma and Doc were frightened of Slim.

Ma stopped prowling. She stared at Doc.

"I could give her something," Doc said. He looked appealingly at Ma. "I don't like doing it, Ma, but we just can't keep her here any longer."

Ma hesitated.

"Would Slim know?"

"He couldn't prove anything," Doc said. "She'd die in her sleep. He—he'd find her dead."

Ma looked at the desk clock.

"He'll be back in a couple of hours." She stood hesitating, looking from Eddie to Doc and back to Eddie again.

"We've got to do it, Ma," Eddie said.

Ma sat down. Her great hands turned into fists.

"Yes, we've got to do it." She looked at Doc. "You fix it, Doc. When you've done it, get out and stay away until late. Let him find her. I'll tell him I haven't been near her. You keep away too, Eddie."

Eddie drew in a long deep breath. It would be all right now, he was thinking. Once the Blandish girl was dead, Anna could come back to the club.

Doc stood, hesitating, sweating and scared.

"Get going," Ma said to him. "The sooner it's done now, the better. Don't sit there like an old fool. This had to happen. Get going."

Doc got slowly to his feet and went out of the room.

"And you get out," Ma said to Eddie. "I don't want you around until ten tonight. Go to a movie or something, but keep out of the way."

"Okay, Ma," Eddie said and started for the door, then he paused. "When she's gone, it'll be okay for Anna to work here, Ma?"

"Yes, it'll be okay," Ma said.

She moved slowly to her desk and sat down. Eddie watched her.

"I'll have to find Slim another girl," Ma said. "He's got the taste for girls now."

Eddie grimaced.

"That won't be so easy," he said.

Ma's face crinkled into a cynical smile.

"I'll find someone," she said. "You can do anything if you have enough money."

Eddie went out. He saw Doc Williams going up the stairs. He was glad he hadn't to do the job. He felt sorry for the Blandish girl. She had had a tough break. As he walked across the courtyard to where he had parked his car, he was thinking she would be better off dead anyway.

He got into his car. There was a movie he wanted to see. He'd take a look at it, then he would pick Anna up for dinner.

As he drove away, two detectives, acting on Brennan's instructions, took up positions where they could watch the entrance of the club without being seen.

4

Slim stood at the foot of the stairs looking up at Ma.

Flynn and Woppy were behind and to the right of Slim. There was an expression on Ma's face that Flynn had never seen before. He had never thought of Ma as being old. It came as a shock to him now as he looked at her to realize just how old she was.

Slim knew something bad had happened. He too had never seen this slack, defeated look on Ma's raddled face. "What's the matter?" he demanded. "What are you looking like that for?"

Ma didn't say anything. One of her great hands rested on the banister rail, gripping it so tightly her knuckles were white.

"Say something!" Slim yelled at her. "What's the matter?"

Ma thought: when I tell him, he'll kill me. If only Eddie was here. Eddie is the only one who has the guts to stop him. Flynn won't. Flynn will stand by and watch him kill me.

She found herself saying in a cold, flat voice, "The girl's gone."

Slim stiffened. He leaned forward to peer up at Ma, his thin lips lifting off his discolored teeth.

"You're lying," he said. "You've done something to her, haven't you?"

"She's gone," Ma said. "I went into her room a couple of hours ago—she wasn't there."

Slim started up the stairs. Ma watched him come. When he reached her, she stared fixedly at him.

"You old cow," Slim snarled. "You're trying to frighten me, but I don't scare easily. If you've touched her, I'll kill you. I told you, didn't I? Anyone who touches her has me to reckon with."

"She's gone," Ma repeated.

Slim went past her, and down the passage. He pushed open the door and went into the sitting room. He looked around, then entered die bedroom.

Ma waited. Her sagging face glistened with sweat. She could hear Slim moving from room to room. Flynn said, "How did she get away, Ma?" Ma looked down at him. She saw the stark fear on his face. "I don't know. I went in there. She had gone."

"Where's Doc?" Woppy asked, a quaver in his voice.

"He's gone," Ma said. "You had better go too. We're washed

up. This is the end of the road. The cops will have her by now."

"If they had her," Flynn said, "they would be here by now." He started up the stairs as Slim came out into the passage. Slim had his knife in his hand. His yellow eyes were gleaming. Flynn paused, half way up the stairs, staring at Slim who moved silently and slowly towards Ma.

"You've killed her, haven't you?" Slim said. "You always wanted to be rid of her. All right... so you killed her. Now, it's my turn. I'm going to kill you."

"I haven't touched her," Ma said, as motionless as a statue. "Someone took her away. She couldn't have got away by herself. All right, Slim, go ahead and kill me if that's what you want. Then you won't have the girl and you won't have me. Maybe you'll be better off with neither of us."

She was quick to see a sudden flicker of doubt in Slim's gleaming eyes.

"Go ahead," she went on. "See where it gets you. See what it'll be like to be on your own. You've always wanted to be the big shot, haven't you, Slim? But watch out. You won't be able to trust anyone. You'll have to keep under cover. You'll have to find some place to hide." She stared at him. "Where will you hide, Slim?"

The gleaming knife pointing at her wavered. Slim hesitated. He suddenly seemed lost as he looked from Ma to Flynn and back to Ma again.

"What are we going to do, Ma?" he asked. "We've got to find her."

Ma drew in a deep breath. It had been a close thing. Even now she was afraid to move.

A sudden commotion at the Club entrance made them all look around. Flynn's hand dropped on his gun butt.

Doc Williams came panting up the stairs. His face was sweating and purple. He saw Slim standing by Ma, knife in hand. He saw Ma, stiff as a statue: Woppy leaning against the wall, his face the color of dough: Flynn with a half-drawn gun in his hand.

Unsteadily, he walked to the foot of the stairs.

"Rocco's got her!" he said. "Hear that, Ma? That goddamn little wop's got her!"

Slim came down the stairs, shoving Flynn aside so violently

Flynn nearly fell. Slim caught hold of Doc's shirt front and shook him.

"Where is he?" he snarled. "How do you know he's got her?"

Ma came lumbering down the stairs. She caught hold of Slim's wrist and shoved him back.

"Leave him alone," she said, then to Doc, "Let's have it. Are you sure Rocco's got her?"

Doc wiped his sweating face.

"Get me a drink," he said and went over to sit on one of the sofas.

Ma signaled to Woppy, who ran into the bar.

"When I left you, Ma," Doc said. "I was ready to pull out. I felt bad. I had to have a drink. I went to the bar at the corner..."

Woppy came over to him and thrust a tumbler half full of whiskey into his hand. Doc drank greedily, then he set the glass down.

"Get on with it!" Slim snarled.

"I got talking to the barman," Doc said. "He asked me who the redhead was he had seen getting into a taxi with Rocco. I sat like a fool, drinking and talking for over an hour before it jelled. I came right back, Ma. It adds up, doesn't it? Rocco and a redhead. It would be his way of leveling the score."

Slim started towards the exit.

"Wait!" Ma said. "Don't go off half-cocked..."

Slim didn't even look around. He went down the steps, jerked open the door and moved out into the darkening courtyard.

"Go after him," Ma said to Flynn, "and you too, Woppy."

"To hell with him," Flynn said. "I'm getting out of here. I've had enough. Give me some money, Ma. I'm quitting."

"Oh, no you're not," Ma said. "You've got nowhere to quit to, you dope! You're getting no money from me! Go after him and you too, Woppy!"

Flynn hesitated, then cursing under his breath, he jerked his head at Woppy and went down the steps to the door.

When Woppy had followed him out into the darkness, Ma put her hand on Doc's shoulder.

"I thought I'd seen the last of you, Doc," she said. "Now what are you going to do?"

Doc was a little drunk.

"What is there to do? I was going on the run, Ma, but I suddenly realized there was nowhere to run to. He'll bring her back and it'll start all over again."

"He hasn't got her yet," Ma said. "You stick with me, Doc. I'll find a way out of this mess. You stick with me."

5

Miss Blandish lay across Rocco's vast divan, staring with blank eyes up at the ceiling.

At any other time, Rocco would have considered himself well off to have had such a beauty in his room, but now his mind was crawling with alarm, and this long-legged redhead could have been a shop window dummy lying on his bed for all her physical attractions meant to him.

I've got to play this smart, he had told himself when he had persuaded her finally to enter his apartment. It's no good calling the cops. I must contact Blandish. If I'm going to get my hands on that fifteen grand, he is my only hope. If I go to the cops, they'll gyp me out of the money.

He had already checked the telephone book, but Blandish's name wasn't in it. He had called information, but the girl couldn't or wouldn't tell him Blandish's number. When you are a millionaire you don't have your name in the book. This was something Rocco hadn't thought of. Now, after phoning most of the important clubs and restaurants asking for Blandish and getting nowhere, he was getting worried. If he didn't find Blandish soon, he told himself, he could be in trouble. At the back of his mind, he kept thinking of Slim. He couldn't imagine how Slim could possibly guess he had the Blandish girl, but if he did guess and if he did come here, then Rocco knew he wouldn't have long to live.

He had tried to stimulate the girl's memory by giving her the back copies of the newspapers that splashed the kidnapping across their pages. While he had been using the telephone, she had listlessly stared at the newspapers, but he could see she didn't connect herself with the photographs nor with the account of the kidnapping.

He looked over at her. She continued to stare up at the ceiling, her drugged eyes sightless.

"Hey, baby," Rocco said, aware now that they had been in this room for over two hours. "Will you try to concentrate. How can I contact your pa? I've called every lousy number I can think of and still I can't find him."

She moved her long legs as she continued to stare up at the ceiling. She didn't seem to be aware he was in the room.

Exasperated, Rocco went over to her and put his hand on her arm.

"Hey! Wake up!"

The touch of his hand brought a reaction that scared him. She wrenched away and crouched against the wall, her eyes wide with terror.

"Okay, okay," he said soothingly. "You don't have to be scared of me. Will you listen? I'm trying to find your pa. What is his telephone number?"

Miss Blandish cringed away from him.

"Leave me alone." she said. "Don't touch me!"

Rocco tried to control his rising panic.

"If I don't find your pa," he said, "we'll both be in trouble. Don't you understand? We'll have Slim here. How do I find your pa?"

She suddenly slid off the bed and ran to the door. She caught hold of the handle as Rocco reached her.

"Keep away!" she said shrilly. "Let me out of here!"

Sweating, Rocco threw her back onto the bed. He knelt over her, clamping his hand over her mouth.

"Shut up!" he said feverishly. "Do you want Slim to find you?"

She ceased to struggle and for the first time since she had been in the room, her eyes came alive. He took his hand off her mouth.

"Yes, I want Slim," she said. "I want him to come here!"

"You don't know what you're saying," Rocco said, staring at her. "Don't you want to go home? What's the matter with you?"

She shook her head.

"I haven't any home. I haven't anyone. I just want Slim."

Rocco stood up.

"I'm going to call the cops," he said. "I've had enough of this." He went over to the telephone, thinking, if they gyp me out of the reward, it'll be too bad, but I've got to get them here before

Slim gets here.

He began to dial police headquarters. Miss Blandish made a sudden dive off the bed. She caught hold of the telephone cable and yanked it from its terminals.

For a long moment, Rocco, the dead telephone receiver clutched in his hand, stood staring at her, feeling a chill crawling up his spine.

"You crazy fool!" he snarled. "What do you imagine you're doing?"

She backed away from him.

"You must tell him you took me away," she said, wringing her hands. "You must tell him I didn't want to go with you."

"Why, you... you..." Words failed Rocco. "What's the matter with you? I'm trying to help you. Don't you want to get away from Slim?"

She leaned against the wall and she began to cry weakly.

"I can't get away from him. I'll have him with me to the end of my days."

"You're talking crazy!" Rocco cried. "I'm going to fetch the cops."

She slid along the wall to the door and set her back against it.

"No! You must wait here until he comes!" she said, her voice shrill. "You must tell him you took me away!"

Exasperated, Rocco caught hold of her arm and dragged her away from the door. He threw her onto the bed. As he turned to the door, she started up. Her hand closed around a heavy glass ashtray standing on the bedside table. She threw the ashtray at him. It caught him on the side of his head and he went down on his hands and knees, stunned.

Miss Blandish leaned against the wall, staring down at him.

Rocco tried to push himself upright, then he flopped down on his side, holding his head and groaning.

The sound of a door opening made Miss Blandish look across the room. The door leading to the bathroom was opening. She stood transfixed as the door swung fully open and Slim moved into the room.

Slim had come up the fire escape and through the bathroom window. His yellow, gleaming eyes moved from Miss Blandish to Rocco sprawling on the floor.

Only half conscious, Rocco sensed his danger. An instinctive feeling warned him he was but a heart beat away from death. He rolled over on his back, his hands raised in a futile gesture of protection.

Slim came forward. He was grinning.

Miss Blandish saw the glittering knife in his hand and she turned away, closing her eyes.

She heard Rocco whimper.

The sounds that followed made her sink onto her knees, her hands over her ears.

Each dull blow of Slim's knife into Rocco's body made her stiffen and shudder.

6

For two interminable hours, Anna Borg had been locked in an isolated cell below stairs at Police headquarters. She was now both scared and exhausted. During the first hour she had yelled, screamed and cursed but no one had come near her. She felt buried alive and her nerves were rapidly going to pieces.

She kept asking herself why she had been picked up and bustled into this cell. When Eddie had rushed off to talk to Ma about Johnny, Anna had decided to quit. She had had enough of Eddie and the Paradise Club. As soon as she had heard his car drive away, she had thrown some clothes into a suitcase, taken Eddie's store of money he kept in the apartment against an emergency and had taken a taxi to the railroad station.

She had told herself she would go to New York. She knew she could always get some kind of a job in a clip joint until she had time to look around. Anything now seemed better than hanging around with Eddie and getting nowhere with a chance of getting caught up in some trouble with Ma Grisson and her stupid son.

But as she paid off the taxi, two large men stepped up to her from nowhere and one of them flashed a badge at her.

"Anna Borg?"

"You can say 'Miss', can't you?" Anna snapped, glaring at the two detectives. But for all her aggression, she had a sudden cold sinking feeling. Were these baboons going to arrest her?

"Police Chief wants to talk to you, baby," one of the men

said. "Won't keep you long."

A police car slid up. Anna was aware that passersby were pausing and staring.

"I've got a train to catch," she said angrily. "You can tell that egghead to drop dead."

A large hand rested on her arm.

"Come on, baby," the detective said persuasively. "You don't want trouble, do you? It won't take long."

"Take your paw off me!" Anna flared. She stood hesitating, then as the other detective moved forward, she got into the car. The two detectives got in after her and the car shot away. "I'll make trouble for you two," she threatened. "I'll get my lawyer to fix you! You'll be pounding a beat before you know where you are!"

The older of the two detectives laughed.

"Be your age, baby," he said. "Relax."

Anna swore at him, then relapsed into a sullen silence. Fear was nibbling at her. Had they connected her with Alvin Heinie's death? It seemed a long time since she had discovered that Heinie had been staying at her hotel and that he had ratted on Riley. She had gone to his room in a fit of furious impulse and had shot him as he had opened the door. She had regretted the act ever since. But up to this moment she had felt sure the shooting couldn't be traced to her; now she wasn't so sure.

At police headquarters, she had demanded to speak to her lawyer, but the desk sergeant merely gave her a bored, blank stare and waved to a hard-faced wardress who caught hold of her and pushed her, struggling and screaming down a passage and into a dark cell. The door slammed and locked behind her.

The two-hour wait had quieted Anna. When eventually the lock snapped back and the door swung open, she jumped anxiously to her feet.

The wardress beckoned to her.

"Come on," she said. "The Chief's ready to talk to you now."

"Someone's going to pay for this!" Anna said but without much conviction.

She was led up the stairs, through the charge room and into Brennan's office. She came to an abrupt standstill in the doorway when she saw Fenner sitting on the window sill, Brennan behind his desk and two detectives leaning up against the wall. She stared at Fenner, her eyes round.

The wardress gave her a push and she staggered forward a few paces, then she heard the door close behind her.

"You're going to be sorry for this!" Anna yelled at Brennan. "I want my lawyer!"

"Sit down, Anna," Brennan said quietly. "I want to talk to you."

"Where do you get this Anna stuff from?" Anna snapped. "I'm Miss Borg to you."

"Sit down and shut up!" one of the detectives barked.

"Ape!" Anna shrilled, but she sat down, looking uneasily from Brennan to Fenner.

"We have reason to believe that Miss Blandish, the girl kidnapped four months ago, is being held at the Paradise Club," Brennan said.

Anna stared at him. Her face was bewildered.

"Have you gone nuts?" she demanded. "Everyone knows Frankie Riley snatched the girl. What are you getting at?"

"That's what we thought, but we know different now," Brennan went on. "The Grisson gang took the girl from Riley. We're pretty certain she is in the club right now."

"Are you trying to frame Eddie?" Anna said, her eyes narrowing. "Don't expect me to help you, copper. I don't know nothing about any snatch."

Fenner said, "Time marches on, Brennan. Let her see the exhibits. If they don't soften her, nothing will."

Brennan nodded. He signaled to one of the detectives who moved over to Anna.

"Come on, baby. I've got something to show you."

Anna looked uneasily at Brennan.

"I want my lawyer. You can't keep me here..."

"Come on; don't talk so much," the detective said.

Anna got to her feet. She followed the detective out of the room. Fenner and Brennan exchanged glances.

"I don't think she knows anything," Brennan said. "We could be wasting our time."

"We can but try," Fenner said and lit a cigarette.

They waited.

After ten minutes or so, the door pushed open and the detective brought Anna back. He was supporting her. Her face was white and her eyes were pools of horror. She dropped limply into the chair and she hid her face in her hands.

"Can you identify him as Riley?" Brennan asked.

She shuddered.

"You dirty sonsofbitches," she said. "How could you do this to me?"

Fenner went over to her.

"He isn't a pretty sight, is he? The Grisson gang did that to him. We found the three of them: Riley, Bailey and Old Sam. It's a sweet setup for Ma Grisson, and what a laugh Eddie must have had when you believed Riley had walked out on you. Riley got the blame for everything and all the time he was dead and buried. Did you get any of the ransom money? I bet you didn't. All you got was a cheap strip job at the club and a tumble from Eddie. Well, here's your chance to even the score. How about it, baby?"

"Get away from me!" Anna screamed at him. "I don't know nothing about nothing!"

"Get smart," Fenner said. "You're in the clear now; keep in the clear. You cooperate with us, and we'll cooperate with you. Now listen, we want to know if the girl's in the club. We think she is, but we've got to know for certain. She's in the locked room upstairs, isn't she?"

White-faced and shaking, Anna glared at him.

"Find out for yourself!"

"Put yourself in that girl's place!" Brennan said, leaning across his desk. "How would you like to be shut up with a moron like Grisson? Come on, Anna, if you know anything, spill it. There's a fifteen grand reward, and I'll see you get it."

"Oh, drop dead!" Anna said viciously. "I've never squealed to a copper and I'm not starting now!"

Fenner said, "Can I talk to this baby alone for five minutes?"

Brennan hesitated, then he got to his feet. Time was pressing. He went out of the room, jerking his head at the two detectives who followed him out.

Anna faced Fenner.

"You're wasting your breath," she said. "I've got nothing to tell you."

"I think you have," Fenner said. "Anyway, I've something to

tell you. I've been checking up on you. Brennan doesn't know you had a room at the Palace Hotel on the night Alvin Heinie was shot to death. He doesn't know you own a .25 automatic, but he does know Heinie was shot with a .25. It wouldn't take him long to put two and two together and slap a murder charge on you if I told him what I'm telling you. You had the motive, the opportunity and the gun. You cooperate with me and I'll keep my mouth shut, otherwise I'm going to tip Brennan off that you were at the hotel that night and then he'll really work you over."

Anna's eyes shifted.

"How about it?" Fenner asked. "We're wasting time. Is the Blandish girl in the club?"

Anna hesitated, then she said, "I don't know, but there is a girl in that room. I've never seen her. I don't know if she's the girl or not."

Fenner went to the door and called Brennan in.

"She's had a change of mind," he said. "She knows there is a girl in the locked room, but she hasn't seen her."

"How do you know there's a girl there if you haven't seen her?" Brennan demanded.

"I've heard the boys talk," Anna said sullenly. "I've seen Ma go up there with stuff from the laundry. I've seen Slim go in there with packages from women's stores."

"Now start using your brains," Brennan said. "How do we bust in there and get to the girl before she gets hurt?"

Anna shrugged.

"Search me. I'm not running your stinking police force. That's your job."

"When the club's open, what are the chances of rushing the place?" Fenner asked.

"Not a chance. They've really got that end organized. Every member is known. Until they identify themselves, the door's not opened."

"Is there any other way in?"

"I don't know of one."

Brennan and Fenner exchanged glances. Fenner shrugged.

"Okay," Brennan said. He went to the door and called the wardress. "Take her to Doyle's office and sit with her."

"Hey!" Anna exclaimed, jumping to her feet. "You're not keeping me here! Now listen..."

"You're staying here until we get die girl," Brennan said. "Take her away."

Protesting loudly, Anna was pushed out of the room. When her yells had died away down the passage, Brennan said. "She's told us exactly nothing."

"Except there is a girl in the locked room," Fenner said, "and it can't be anyone else but the Blandish girl, but how do we get her out?"

"If we're going to bust in there," Brennan said, "we've got to make sure none of the club members are there. The first move is to cordon off the joint and stop anyone going in. The club opens around ten o'clock," He looked at his watch. "It's not yet eight. If we could pick up one of the Grisson gang, we might be able to persuade him to talk. There may be another way into the club besides through that steel door." He picked up the telephone receiver. "That you, Doyle? I want one of the Grisson gang, and I want him fast. No, I don't care who it is. Get them all if you can, but I want at least one in a hurry. Okay." He hung up. "If any of those rats are floating around town, we'll have them. There's not much else we can do now except wait."

"We should tell Blandish what's cooking," Fenner said. "After all, she's his daughter."

Brennan hesitated, then nodded. He waved to the telephone.

"Okay: go ahead and tell him," he said.

7

Eddie Schultz discovered he wasn't as tough as he imagined he was. Although the movie he was watching had plenty of action, it didn't hold his interest.

He kept thinking of Miss Blandish. She would be dead by now, he told himself. What would Ma do with the girl's body? He guessed that would be a lousy job for him and Flynn to handle. How would Slim react? Eddie thought he wouldn't be in Ma's shoes for any money.

Suddenly he couldn't stand the darkness of the movie house any longer. He got up and pushing his way roughly past the three people between him and the aisle, he walked to the exit. The time was three minutes past eight. He needed a drink.

Crossing the street, he went into a bar, ordered a double Scotch, then went over to a telephone booth and called his apartment. He would tell Anna to join him at the bar, and they would have an early dinner together. He didn't feel like sharing his own company any longer. He was irritated when he got no answer. It was unusual for Anna to leave the apartment before nine. Where had she got to? He went back to the bar, tossed off the drink, paid for it and left the bar. He decided he'd drive over to his apartment. Maybe Anna had slipped out for a moment and would be back.

He reached his apartment, parked his car and entered the apartment lobby.

The janitor, a heavily built Negro, was sitting in his office, reading the racing sheet.

"Hi, Curly," Eddie said, pausing, "did you see Miss Borg go out?"

The janitor lowered his newspaper.

"Sure did, Mr. Schultz. She went out ten minutes after you did." He squinted at Eddie curiously. "She had a suitcase with her."

Eddie frowned.

"Okay, Curly." He crossed to the elevator and rode up to his apartment, unlocked the door and entered. He went into the bedroom. The closet doors stood wide open. He saw at a glance most of Anna's clothes were missing.

He swore under his breath. So she had skipped! Should he tell Ma? He hesitated. Ma would have to know. He crossed over to the telephone as the front doorbell rang.

Who could this be? he asked himself uneasily. His hand slid inside his coat and his fingers closed over the butt of his gun. He went to the door.

"Who is it?" he called.

"A message from Miss Borg, Mr. Schultz," the janitor called.

Hurriedly, Eddie unlocked the door which smashed open as he turned the handle, sending him reeling back into the room. Before he could recover his balance, two big men had piled into the room and were covering him with guns.

"Take it easy, Schultz," one of them said. "Just keep your hands still."

The janitor, his eyes rolling, peered into the room, then he turned and hurried away.

Eddie faced the detectives.

"You've got nothing on me," he said, a cold uneasy feeling in his stomach. "What's the big idea—busting in like this?"

One of the big men moved around him and took away his gun.

"Got a permit for this, Schultz?" he asked.

Eddie didn't say anything.

"Come on. Don't let's have any trouble. If you want it, you can have plenty of it, but why want it?"

"I'm not coming with you," Eddie snarled. "You've got nothing on me."

"The same old story," the detective said. "Let's go." Eddie hesitated, then he let the two men shove him into the elevator and down to the waiting police car. Ten minutes later, he was facing Brennan and Fenner in Brennan's office.

"What's the big idea?" Eddie blustered. "You've no right to bring me here. I want my lawyer."

"Show him the exhibits," Brennan said, "then bring him back."

Shrugging, Eddie swaggered out with the two detectives, but he felt far from swaggering. Why had they picked up Anna? Just how much did Anna know? Had she talked?

Five minutes later, he was back in front of Brennan, white-faced and shaking.

"We know you and your pals knocked those guys off," Brennan said. "Johnny talked before he was hit. We know you and your pals snatched the Blandish girl. You have a chance to save your dirty hide, Schultz. We want the girl out of the club. You tell us how we get her out and I'll see you keep out of the gas chamber. You'll go away for ten to fifteen, but you'll save your goddamn hide. Is it a deal?"

"I don't know what you're talking about, copper," Eddie said, sweat running down his face. "I didn't snatch the girl... I didn't kill those guys. I want my lawyer."

"I haven't time to argue with you, Schultz," Brennan said. "Your only hope is to come clean, and you'd better come clean fast or else you'll wish you were never born."

"I tell you I don't know a thing!" Eddie shouted. "I want my lawyer."

Brennan picked up the telephone receiver. "Send O'Flagherty and Doogan up here right away," he said and as he replaced the receiver, he went on to Eddie, "These two guys have been pushed around badly by gangsters like you. O'Flagherty was in hospital for four months and Doogan lost an eye. We keep them on the force because they wouldn't know what to do with themselves if we didn't, they're not much use for active service, but they do have their uses. They hate gangsters. Every now and then I get a tough bird like you who won't cooperate with me. I hand him over to these two guys and they love to have him. I don't inquire what they do to him, but invariably he talks after being with them for a couple of hours or less. He invariably looks a hell of a mess when he comes back here to do his talking, but that doesn't worry me because my two boys were in a hell of a mess when we found them after the gangsters had worked them over."

Eddie had heard about O'Flagherty and Doogan. He knew some of the boys had beaten up the two detectives, and at the time, he had rubbed his hands gleefully at the news, but the idea of having these two apes work him over appalled him.

"You can't do this to me!" he exclaimed, backing up against the wall. "I've got friends! You touch me and I'll see you lose your job."

Brennan grinned wolfishly.

"All you rats say the same thing—I'm still here."

The door bounced open and two men came in. Eddie had never seen men as big as these two with the exception of professional heavyweights. They were dressed in sweat shirts and blue slacks. The sight of their enormous, rolling muscles and their hard, brutal faces turned him cold.

They stood by the door, looking at him. Doogan, whose empty red eye socket seemed to glare directly at Eddie, folded enormous hands into fists. O'Flagherty, his face scarred, his nose flattened, looked expectantly at Brennan.

"Boys," Brennan said, "this is Eddie Schultz. We know he's connected with the kidnapping of the Blandish girl. He says there's no one on this pansy police force who can make him talk. Do you want to have a try at him?"

O'Flagherty showed his broken teeth in a grin. He eyed Eddie the way a tiger might eye a fat goat.

"Sure, Captain," he said. "We would like a try. He doesn't look so tough."

Doogan walked up to Eddie.

"Are you tough, baby?" he asked, peering at Eddie with his one eye. His right hand whizzed up and slapped Eddie across his face. It was as if he had been hit with a sledge hammer. He rocketed across the room and went down on his hands and knees, his head spinning, his face on fire.

"Hey! Not in my goddamn office!" Brennan protested. "I don't want blood all over the place. Get him out of here!" Eddie pushed himself to his feet. His nerve cracked as Doogan and O'Flagherty closed in on him.

"Call them off!" he yelled. "I'll talk! Don't let them touch me!"

"Hold it, boys," Brennan said and got to his feet.

The two policemen drew back, gaping in astonishment and disappointment at Eddie.

"I'll talk," Eddie repeated, holding his bruised, flaming cheek. "Don't let them touch me."

"Well, this is a surprise," Brennan said. "Okay, boys, wait outside. If I think he needs loosening up, I'll call you."

Doogan wiped his nose with the back of his hand in a gesture of disgust.

"Can I hit him once more, Captain?" he asked hopefully, doubling his fists.

Eddie backed away, shielding his face with his hands.

"Not right now," Brennan said. "Maybe later."

Reluctantly, the two policemen went out.

"Sit down," Brennan said.

Eddie sank into a chair, facing Brennan.

"Is the Blandish girl in the club?" Brennan asked.

Eddie licked his lips.

"Is that deal still on, Captain? You keep me out of the gas box?"

"It's still on. Is she in there?"

"Yeah."

"How do we get to her?"

Eddie hesitated, then he blurted out, "She's dead, Captain. There was nothing I could do about it. It was Ma. She made Doc knock her off."

Both Fenner and Brennan got to their feet.

"Are you lying?" Brennan asked in a cold, harsh voice.

"I tell you it was nothing to do with me," Eddie said frantically. "Ma always wanted to get rid of the girl, but Slim fell for her. Then we heard this guy was going to talk to Johnny and Ma sent Slim and the boys to fix Johnny. While Slim was out of the way, Ma decided to knock the girl off. I tried to stop her, but you can't do a goddamn thing with Ma once she's made up her mind. She told Doc to give the girl a shot."

Brennan and Fenner exchanged glances. Fenner made a gesture of helplessness. All along, he had expected to hear Miss Blandish was dead: this came as no surprise to him.

"Is there another way into the club except past that steel door?" Brennan asked.

"Through the warehouse next door," Eddie said. "There's a door in the wall on the left as you go in."

Brennan yelled for Doogan.

"Take this rat down to the cells," he said as Doogan came in, "and lay off him, do you hear?"

Doogan grabbed hold of Eddie and hustled him out.

Fenner said, "Maybe it's the best thing. Even her old man hoped she would be dead. I'd better tell him."

"Yeah. Well, I'll fix that old bitch of a woman. Do you want to come along?"

"I'll be along. I'll call Blandish first."

As Fenner reached for the telephone, Brennan ran out, yelling instructions to the riot squad sergeant.

CHAPTER FIVE

1

Miss Blandish leaned against the wall, biting her knuckles because she couldn't scream and because she wanted to. She stared in horror at Rocco as he lay on the ornate rug. From the many wounds inflicted on him, blood made snake-like bands across the floor.

Slim stood over him, breathing heavily, his blood-stained knife dangling between his slack fingers. He bent over Rocco and wiped his knife clean on the dead man's coat.

"He won't bother you again," he said and grinned at Miss Blandish. "So long as I'm around, no one will ever bother you."

He went over to the window and looked down in the street. The traffic was heavy and people were crowding the sidewalks, going home. He realized he couldn't show himself with the girl on the streets. She could easily be recognized. He wondered how Ma would cope with this situation. He glanced over at Rocco, then an idea occurred to him. He was immediately pleased with himself. He'd show Ma she wasn't the only one with brains.

He crossed to the closet, opened it and pulled out one of Rocco's suits. He found a shirt and tie. He threw the clothes on the divan.

"Put those on," he said to Miss Blandish. "I've got to get you home somehow. Go on, get into that rig."

Miss Blandish shook her head and backed away. Impatiently, Slim pulled her to the divan.

"Do what I say!" he said, pinching her arm. "Put 'em on!"

Fearfully and reluctantly, she peeled the cheap cotton dress over her head and let it drop to the floor. Then she hurriedly reached for the shirt, aware that Slim was watching her.

They looked at each other. She read the message in his eyes, and clutching the shirt to her, she backed away.

"No... please..."

Slim shuffled over to her and snatched the shirt from her.

His mouth was pursed, his breathing suddenly violent, his eyes blank.

Shuddering and unresisting, she let him lead her to the divan.

The clock on the mantel ticked busily. The minute hand crawled on across the ornate clock face. A large bluebottle fly buzzed excitedly over the bloodstain on Rocco's coat. The traffic in the street below halted, moved on with a grinding of gears, then halted again.

Miss Blandish gave a sudden sharp cry.

As the minutes passed, the shadows in the room lengthened. Someone in the apartment below turned on a television set. An impersonal voice began to give loud instructions on how to bake a cake. The insistent, domineering voice woke Slim who slowly opened his eyes. He turned his head to look at Miss Blandish, lying flat on her back by his side. She was staring sightlessly up at the ceiling.

"That punk makes it sound like a cake is the most important thing in the world," Slim said. He raised his head to look at the clock. The time was twenty minutes past eight. This surprised him. He hadn't realized he had slept for so long. He got off the bed. The sounds of the traffic had died down. The rush hour home had passed.

"We've got to go," he said. "Ma'll be wondering where we are. Come on, baby, get into that rig."

The girl got off the bed, moving like a sleepwalker. She put on Rocco's shirt and suit. She had trouble fixing the tie. Slim, sitting on the bed, watched her with childish amusement.

"Sort of different, isn't it?" he said. "I used to have trouble with a tie. You get used to it. You look pretty good as a boy." He glanced at Rocco's dead body. "He was a jockey. I got no time for guys who fool around with horses." He kicked Rocco gently. "He got what was coming to him."

Miss Blandish was dressed now. Rocco's suit fitted her quite well. Slim looked at her, nodding his approval.

"You make a fine boy," he said. He stood up and went to the closet and found one of Rocco's hats. "Put this on; hide your pretty hair. You could be my kid brother."

She let him put the hat on her head, standing like a lifeless doll, but cringing a little every time his damp, hot fingers touched her skin.

"Come on," Slim said, "let's go."

He led her into the bathroom, paused to look out of the window down into the yard below, satisfied himself there was no one about, then helped the girl through the window onto the escape.

They went down the escape, Slim holding her arm and pushing her down quickly. On the last stage, a man looked out of the window as they passed. He was fat, balding and elderly.

"Hey! What do you think you're doing?" he demanded.

Slim looked at him, his yellow eyes gleaming. The man stepped back hurriedly. Slim's pale thin face, his loose mouth and gleaming eyes, his long, unkempt hair hanging from under his hat scared the man silly.

Slim had parked the Buick at the end of the alley. He hustled Miss Blandish to the car and pushed her in. He went around to the driver's seat and got in. He paused to open the glove compartment and to take out the .45 that was always kept there. He put the gun under his right thigh, then he started the car and drove into the main street.

As he headed for the club, the wail of a police siren made him stiffen. He looked into the driving mirror. He saw the traffic behind him pulling over to the right, clearing a broad lane in the middle of the road. He too pulled to the right as he saw three police cars come storming up behind him. They flashed past him. Wondering uneasily where they were going, he followed on behind. After a few minutes, he suddenly realized they were slowing down to stop outside the entrance to the courtyard of the Paradise Club.

In sudden panic, he swung the Buick into a side street, cutting across an overtaking car that braked with a violent scream of tires. He pulled up and looked back in time to see a dozen policemen spill out of the cars and run across the courtyard to the club.

He felt sweat on his face. What was he to do? Where was he to go? He looked at Miss Blandish who was staring blankly through the windshield. He felt lost and scared without Ma and the steel door and shutters of the club. His sluggish mind tried to cope with the situation.

"Hey, you!"

He looked to his right. A cop was looking into the car, first at Slim and then at Miss Blandish. Slim recognized him. He was the patrolman of the district: a big, fiery-faced Mick who always pushed the Grisson gang around when he had the chance.

"I want you," the cop said and his hand slid to his gun holster.

Slim's hand dropped on the hidden .45, lifted it and fired in one quick fluent movement. The slug hit the cop in the middle of his chest, throwing him half across the sidewalk.

Miss Blandish screamed. Startled, Slim swung his hand in a backhand slap, hitting her across the mouth, jerking her hard back against the car seat.

Several passersby flattened themselves on the sidewalk.

Swearing, Slim dropped his gun onto the car seat, then started the car and pulled away, accelerating as a man yelled after him.

Slim was vicious in his fear. His one thought was to get onto the open road where he could use the vast speed of the car.

Fenner and Brennan were just leaving a newly arrived police car as Slim shot the cop. The sound of the gun going off made both men pause. They saw the Buick tearing down the street, scattering other cars.

Fenner ran to the dead cop while Brennan signaled to three motorcycle cops to go after the Buick. They went away with roaring exhausts. Then Brennan joined Fenner who shook his head.

"He's gone," he said. "Who could that have been?"

"One of the Grisson gang," Brennan said grimly. "Come on, let's get at the rest of them. That rat won't get far."

More police were arriving. The street was becoming congested with a gaping crowd.

Inside the club, Ma Grisson watched the activity going on outside through one of the peepholes in the steel shutter that covered her office window.

Flynn peered through another peephole. Woppy cowered against the wall. Doc Williams sat near Ma's desk. He had a glass half full of neat whiskey in his hand: his face was shiny with sweat, his eyes glassy.

Ma turned slowly and looked first at Doc and then at Woppy. Flynn stepped back, looking at her.

"Well, here it is," Ma said in a cold hard voice. "This is the end of the road. I don't have to tell you what's ahead of us."

Flynn was cool. His small, flat eyes were restless, but he didn't look afraid. Woppy seemed on the point of collapse. His eyes rolled with terror. Doc took a swig from his glass, shrugging his shoulders. He was too drunk to have any emotions.

Ma plodded across the room, opened a closet and took out a Thompson machine gun.

"You guys can please yourselves," she said. "I know what I'm going to do. Those coppers won't take me alive. I'll get a hell of a bang taking a few of the bastards with me."

Flynn joined her. He too took a machine gun from the closet.

"I'm with you, Ma," he said. "Let's make it quick and gory."

There came a hammering on the steel door. Then a voice, magnified by a loudspeaker bawled, "Come on out, you in there! Come on out with your hands in the air!"

"They'll take some time to bust in," Ma said. She went to her desk and sat down. She put the Thompson on the desk, pointing towards the door. "Okay, boys, leave me. This is my room and this is where I want to die. You find your own holes. Go on... beat it."

Doc said, "Why not let them in?" He finished his whiskey and set the glass down on the desk. "We have money, Ma. We can hire the best lawyers. We still have a chance."

Ma smiled contemptuously.

"Do you think so? You poor old drunken fool! Go ahead if you feel that way about it. Find yourself a lawyer and see where he gets you. I know better. Just get out of here and leave me alone."

Flynn had already gone. He ran through the dark restaurant to the stairs. The sound of hammering on the steel door made him pause in the lobby. He looked around, then he slid behind the counter guarding the stairs. He rested his Thompson on the counter and waited, his heart thumping, his thin lips screwed off his teeth in a vicious grin.

Woppy came charging out into the lobby. He looked like a rabbit hunted by a fox. As he started towards the front entrance, Flynn yelled at him, "Don't do it or I'll cut you to pieces!"

Woppy spun around and glared frantically at Flynn.

"I've got to get out of here!" he yammered. "I don't want to get killed! I just want to get out of here!"

"You've got nowhere to go now," Flynn said. "You have no future either. Come here."

A gun banged behind Flynn. Woppy's face suddenly became a crimson smear. He fell forward and rolled over, his hands clawing the air.

Crouching, Flynn spun around. Above him at the head of the stairs, two cops had appeared guns in hand.

As Flynn nipped back the trigger of the Thompson, he realized the cops had found a way into the club through the warehouse and this was indeed the end of the road.

The Thompson hammered out its message of death. The two cops seemed to dissolve under the hail of lead. Then another Thompson started up from somewhere above the stairs.

Flynn crouched down as a sheet of lead swept just above his head. He was sweating and grinning, thinking this was the way to die—hit and be hit.

He twisted around, lifted the barrel of his gun and peered around the edge of his cover. The Thompson above yammered out its deadly, roaring note. Four slugs took the top of Flynn's head off. He was firing back as he slumped down onto the carpet in a mess of blood and brains.

Four cops moved cautiously into sight. They looked down into the lobby. Brennan joined them.

"That leaves Doc, the old woman and Slim," Brennan said as Fenner came up.

"One of them got away in the Buick," Fenner reminded him. "Could have been Slim."

Brennan moved out into the open. Cupping his mouth with his hands, he bawled, "Hey, you! Come on out! You haven't a chance! Come out with your hands in the air!"

Doc Williams pushed himself out of his chair.

"Well, Ma, as you said, this is the end of the road. I'm no fighting man. I'm going to give myself up."

Seated behind her desk, her big hands on the machine gun, Ma grinned at him, showing her yellow teeth.

"Suit yourself," she said. "They'll send you away for life or they'll even put you in the gas chamber. It would be better to go quick."

"I'm no fighting man," Doc repeated. "So long, Ma. It looked good, didn't it? But you remember all along I said I didn't like kidnapping. See what's come of it."

"Come, on out, you in there!" Brennan bawled. "This is the last time! Come on out or we'll come on in!"

"So long, Doc," Ma said. "Go out slow with your hands in the air. Those guys sound trigger happy."

Doc turned and walked slowly to the door. He opened it and then paused.

"I'm coming," he called. "Don't shoot."

Ma grinned contemptuously. She lifted the Thompson and aimed it at Doc's back.

As Doc began to move out into the dimly lit restaurant, Ma squeezed the trigger. The gun fired one quick, violent burst and Doc was thrown forward. He slid to the ground, dead before he hit the carpet.

"You'll be better off dead, you poor old fool," Ma said and she got to her feet. Holding the machine gun in both hands, she moved silently and steadily to the door. At the door, she paused.

"Come and get me!" she yelled. "Come on, you yellow punks! Come and get me!"

2

Gripping the steering wheel, Slim leaned forward, staring with fixed concentration as he drove the Buick at a furious speed down the main road out of the city. His loose mouth hung open; his pale dirty skin shone with sweat. He could hear the wailing sirens as the motorcycle cops chased him. In another mile he would be on the main highway and if he could once get there he was sure the souped-up engine of the Buick would outstrip anything coming after him.

A car came out fast from a side turning. A crash seemed inevitable. Miss Blandish cried out, shielding her face. Grinning, Slim stamped down on the gas pedal as the other driver frantically braked. The Buick swept past with inches to spare.

A hundred yards further on there was a main intersection and as the Buick roared towards the intersection the green lights flicked to red.

Slim put his hand down on the horn button. The motorcycle

cops, seeing he wasn't going to stop, opened up then-sirens to warn crossing traffic to get out of the way.

The Buick shot across the intersection as the traffic squealed to a standstill. One driver wasn't quick enough. The Buick caught his wing a glancing blow, smashing his offside headlamp.

Slim, cursing, steadied the Buick with a twist of the wheel and kept on. Then suddenly he was on the freeway. He relaxed slightly, squeezing down on the gas pedal, feeling the big car surge forward.

The light was fading now. In a few minutes it would be dark. The wailing sound of the sirens irritated him. He was pretty sure they wouldn't catch him now he could use his superior speed. He glanced in the driving mirror. About two hundred yards behind he could see two of the motorcycle cops, leaning over their handlebars, belting after him. The third cop had disappeared. He saw a sudden flash and then heard a bang. One of the cops was firing at him. Slim snarled to himself.

"Get down on the floor," he said to Miss Blandish. "Go on—do what I say!"

Shaking, she slid off the seat and onto the floor. He flicked on his sidelights. At least the sirens behind him were keeping the road clear. Traffic coming into the city had slowed and was pulling to one side. One of the cops had fallen back, but the other kept after him.

Slim suddenly eased his foot on the gas pedal. The Buick lost speed. Watching in the mirror, Slim saw the lone cop surging up behind him. Slim waited, his face a vicious snarl. The cop drew alongside, yelling something which Slim couldn't hear above the noise of the motorcycle engine. Grinning, Slim swerved the Buick violently. He felt the side of the car hit the motorcycle. He wrestled madly with the wheel, trying to keep out of a skid. Out of the corner of his eye he saw the motorcycle careening across the road. It hit the verge and disappeared in a cloud of dust.

Slim righted the Buick and shoved down the gas pedal. The car tore on into the gathering darkness. Without the distracting sound of the pursuing siren, Slim was able to consider what to do.

He was on the run, he told himself. He was out in the open.

The girl was going to be poison from now on, but he didn't for a moment consider getting rid of her.

He glanced at the gas gauge. He had plenty of gas. But where to go? He could think of no one who would hide him. He reached down and touched Miss Blandish on her shoulder.

"Come on up," he said. "It's okay now."

Miss Blandish struggled back on the seat beside him. She crouched away from him, staring through the windshield at the long, wide road that stretched endlessly in front of them.

She had had no drugs now for fifteen hours and her mind was slowly clearing. She tried to remember what she was doing in this racing car. Dimly, at the back of her mind, she had a picture of a small, dark man with blood on his coat.

"They'll come after us," Slim said. "They'll hunt us. You and me are in this together to the end. We've got nowhere to go."

Miss Blandish didn't understand what he was saying. She just felt a cold sick feeling of fear at the sound of his voice.

Slim shrugged. He was used to her silences, but he wished she would talk now. He wished she would help him. He knew before very long the cops would be setting up road blocks and the highway wouldn't be safe. He would have to get off the highway and get lost in the country. He wished Ma was with him. She would know what to do.

A few miles further on he came to an intersection and he left the highway, driving along a secondary road for another few miles until he came to a dirt road. He swung the Buick off the secondary road and drove up the twisting hilly dirt road that led quickly to wooded country.

By now it was dark and Slim became aware he was hungry. After driving for several miles, he spotted ahead of him the lights of a farmhouse. He slowed down, then seeing the open farm gate, he swung the Buick up the rutted track leading to the farmhouse.

"I'm going to get some food," he said. "You wait in the car." He put his damp hot hand on Miss Blandish's wrist.

"Don't run away, baby. You and me have got to stick together now. You sit quiet."

He stopped the car and got out. Taking his gun, he walked silently to the lighted window and peered in.

Three people sat at the table: a thickset man of around fifty in a checked shirt and blue jeans, a thin-faced woman who was probably his wife and a fair girl of about twenty, probably his daughter. They were eating and the sight of the meal spread out on the table made Slim's mouth water.

He moved to the door, gently turned the handle and pushed. The door yielded.

The three at the table looked up as he pushed the door wide open. Slim grinned to see the sudden fear on their faces. He showed them the gun, his yellow eyes gleaming.

"Sit still and you won't get hurt," he said.

He moved into the room as the man half started up, only to sink back on his chair as Slim swung the gun in his direction.

"I'll take this," Slim said reaching out and picking up the remains of a meat pie from the table. "You got a phone?"

The man nodded his head to where a telephone stood on a table by the wall. Slim backed to it. He put down the pie and then jerked the cable of the telephone from its socket.

"You all relax," he said. "Just forget you've seen me." He looked at the girl, his eyes running over her figure. She was about Miss Blandish's size. "You!" The gun pointed at her. "Gimme that dress you've got on. Hurry it up!"

The girl went white. She looked at her father.

"One of you want to get shot?" Slim snarled.

"Do it," the man said.

The girl stood up, unzipped the dress and took it off. She was shaking so badly she could hardly stand.

"Throw it here," Slim said.

The girl threw the dress at him. He caught it and tucked it under his arm.

"Just take it easy," he said. He picked up the pie and backed into the darkness. He hurried to the Buick and got in.

Miss Blandish cringed away from him as he tossed the dress into her lap.

"Here's something for you." He set the pie down carefully between them, then started the car. "It'll fit. When we get away from here, you put it on. I don't like seeing you in that punk's suit."

He drove a mile or so up the road, then stopped the car. He looked back along the road, but could see no following lights nor did he hear anything to worry him.

"Come on: let's eat," he said. "It smells good."

He scooped up some of the pie in his dirty fingers and began to eat. Miss Blandish sat huddled away from him.

"Come on," he said impatiently. "It's good."

"No."

He shrugged and went on wolfing the pie down. In five minutes he had finished it and he threw the empty pie dish into the darkness.

"That's better." He wiped his greasy fingers on his trousers' leg. "You get into that dress. Go on... hurry it up!"

"I don't want to."

He caught hold of her by the back of her neck and shook her.

"Do what I tell you!" His voice became high pitched with sudden rage. "Get into it!"

He pushed her out of the car, still holding her by the back of her neck.

"You want me to strip those clothes off you?"

"No."

He let go of her.

"Get on with it!"

In the light of the roof lamp of the Buick, he watched her struggle out of Rocco's suit and put on the dress. He picked up the suit and tossed it into the back of the car. He pushed Miss Blandish back in her seat. She leaned forward, her head in her hands. She was shaking. Her body was now craving for the numbing bliss of the drug Doc gave her regularly. Misty pictures that had haunted her mind during the past four months were gradually coming into focus.

Slim looked uneasily at her. He guessed what was happening to her. He had seen junkies in prison blow their tops because they had been deprived of drugs. If only he could have a word with Ma. She would tell him what to do. Then a disturbing thought entered his head. What had happened to Ma? Had she got away? Had she been trapped in die club? All his life he had regarded her as indestructible. He couldn't believe anything really bad could ever happen to her.

The dirt road abruptly ended at a secondary road and once again Slim found himself driving on a road with other traffic. This worried him. There wasn't much traffic, but every now and then he overtook a truck or a car and he wondered if the Buick would be recognized.

A little later he came upon a small filling station standing at the junction of another dirt road that cut across the secondary road. He swung the car onto the dirt road, then pulled up. He looked back at the filling station. He could see a man sitting in the lighted office reading a newspaper. There would be a telephone in there, Slim thought. He had to get news of Ma. Who could he ask? He remembered Pete Cosmos. Cosmos and Eddie Schultz had always been good pals. Maybe Pete would know something.

"I'm going to telephone," he said to Miss Blandish. "You wait here... understand? You wait here for me."

She remained crouched forward, her head in her hands. He could feel the violence of her trembling. He could see in her present state she wasn't capable of standing, let alone running away.

He got out of the car, pushed the .45 into the waistband of his trousers and walked quickly back to the filling station. He went to the office. The man, fat and beefy, glanced up as Slim pushed open the door. His face registered startled surprise when he saw Slim. He got to his feet.

"I want to use your phone, pal," Slim said. "That okay with you?"

There was something about Slim that scared the man.

"Go ahead, "he said. "You want gas too?"

"No... just the telephone." Slim crossed to the desk. "Give me some air, pal."

The man left the office and stood by the pumps. He kept glancing uneasily through the window at Slim and then hopefully up and down the long dark road.

It took Slim several minutes to find the Cosmos Club in the book. He wasn't used to handling a telephone book and he was swearing and sweating by the time he finally tracked down the number.

Pete answered the telephone himself.

"This is Grisson, Pete," Slim said. "Give it to me fast. What's cooking?"

"All hell's broken loose," Pete said as soon as he had got over his first shock of surprise to hear Slim's voice. "Eddie's been picked up. There was a hell of a battle at the club. Woppy, Flynn and Doc were knocked off during the fight." Slim felt his insides contract. Cold sweat dripped from his face onto his hands.

"Never mind about those punks," he snarled. "How about Ma?"

There was a pause on the line. Slim could hear violent swing music from the club band. He could hear Pete's heavy breathing.

"Wake up!" he shouted. "What's happened to Ma?"

"She's gone, Slim. I'm sorry. You can be proud of her. She knocked off four cops before they got her. She fought it out like a goddamn man!"

Slim felt the bile rise in his mouth. His legs sagged. He let go of the receiver and it fell onto the floor.

Ma gone!

He couldn't believe it. He felt suddenly defenseless, lost, trapped.

The sound of an approaching motorcycle engine made him stiffen. He looked quickly through the window. A State trooper, slowing down on his machine drifted past the filling station, heading towards the Buick.

Slim jumped to the door and opened it. The State trooper stopped by the Buick, got off his machine and leaned in through the Buick's window.

Slim drew his gun.

The filling station attendant, who Slim had forgotten, suddenly let out a yell of warning as he saw the gun in Slim's hand.

The State trooper straightened, looking around, his hand dropping onto his gun butt, but he didn't have a chance.

Slim jerked up the .45 and squeezed the trigger. In the silence of the darkness, the bang of the gun was loud and violent. The State trooper went down, knocking over his motorcycle...

Slim spun around snarling, but there was no sign of the attendant. He hesitated, then ran to the Buick. He stepped over the State trooper's body, got in the car as Miss Blandish opened the off side door and made to get out. Slim grabbed her arm and jerked her back. He reached across her and slammed the door shut.

"Stay quiet!" he shouted, his voice shaking with panic and rage. He started the car and then drove furiously up the dirt road, heading for the woods.

The filling-station attendant came out from behind an oil drum. He ran over to the State trooper, bent over him, then turning, he ran back to his office and grabbed up the telephone.

3

Brennan and Fenner were bending over a large-scale map spread out on a desk in the Operations Room at Headquarters when a police officer came over.

"Mr. Blandish is asking for you, sir."

Brennan made an impatient movement.

"I'll handle him," Fenner said, and leaving the room, he followed the officer to one of the waiting rooms.

John Blandish was standing by the window, looking out across the lights of the city. He turned as Fenner came in.

"I got your message," he said curtly. His face was grey and drawn. "What's happening?"

"We're pretty sure your daughter is alive," Fenner said, joining him at the window. "She has been kept at the Paradise Club these past three months. We broke in there not an hour ago. There's evidence she was kept a prisoner there."

Blandish's face hardened.

"What evidence?"

"A suite of rooms; a locked door; women's clothes."

"Where is she then?"

"Grisson got her out of the club just before the raid. She was dressed in a man's suit. Later we had a report that Grisson raided a farmhouse and took a woman's dress. Since then we've lost them for a moment, but we know more or less which way he is heading. He can't get away. Every road is sealed off. As soon as it is light enough we'll have aircraft searching. It's just a matter of time."

Blandish turned away and stared out of the window.

"Alive... after all this time," he murmured. "I had hoped for her sake she was dead."

Fenner didn't say anything. There was a long pause, then

Blandish asked without turning, "Have you anything else to tell me?"

Fenner hesitated. Blandish turned: his eyes were bleak.

"Don't keep anything from me," he said harshly. "Have you anything else to tell me?"

"They have been drugging her," Fenner said, "and Grisson has been living with her. He is a pathological case. She'll need special care when we find her, Mr. Blandish. I've been talking to the M.O. He doesn't want her exposed to any past contacts until he has had a chance to look at her. I'm putting this badly. Perhaps you'd better talk to him. He thinks you shouldn't be there when we do get her. He thinks it would be better for you to wait at home and for us to bring her to you. She'll need some hours to get over the shock of being free and it would be better for this to happen among strangers. Another thing: Grisson won't surrender. We'll have to kill him. It's going to be a tricky business with her with him. You realize..."

"All right, all right," Blandish said impatiently. "You've made your point. I'll wait for her at home." He started for the door, paused and went on, "I understand it was you who found the clue that started the hunt for this man. I'm not forgetting our bargain. When she is returned, you'll get your money. I'll be waiting at my house. Arrange to keep me informed how the hunt is going and when she is found."

"I'll fix that," Fenner said.

Blandish nodded and went out.

Fenner shook his head, then waiting a few seconds to allow Blandish time to get clear, he returned to the Operations room.

He told Brennan what he had said to Blandish and the Chief nodded.

"You're right," he said. "We've just had another lead on this punk." He put his finger on the map. "Ten minutes ago he was here with the girl. He badly wounded a State trooper who spotted the girl and even spoke to her. They got away but we know which way they are heading. We've tightened the cordon. We've called on the Army to help. It can't be long now. I've got the local radio and television network to interrupt their programs warning everyone in the district to look out for the car."

Fenner sat on the edge of the desk. He was surprised that

the prospects of making thirty thousand dollars wasn't giving him the bang it should. He kept thinking of the Blandish girl and what she had suffered at the hands of Grisson.

"You've got a sweet job on your hands when you do finally corner this rat," he said. "As she'll be with him, you won't be able to blast him out."

"I'll worry my head about that when we have cornered him," Brennan said. He accepted a cup of coffee from a police officer.

"Are you still holding Anna Borg?" Fenner asked, taking a cup of coffee from the tray.

"Only until I've got Grisson, then I'm turning her loose. We've got nothing on her," Brennan said. "We sure have made a clean sweep of the Grisson gang. Phew! That old woman! I'll remember her as long as I live. I thought we'd never cut her down. Even with five slugs in her, she kept on shooting until the goddamn gun was empty. I'm glad Slim isn't like her. It's my bet once the pressure's on, he'll crack. I'm relying on that."

Fenner sat down and put his feet up on the desk. "That girl haunts me," he said, frowning. "She's had a hell of a break. Imagine being locked up with that degenerate for four months."

"Yeah." Brennan finished his coffee. "But the drug they were giving her would turn her into a zombie. I'm more sorry for her right now. The effects of the drug must be wearing off. After an experience like this, I doubt if she'll ever be a hundred percent normal."

"Her old man thinks the same," Fenner said. "I could tell by the way he spoke. She'd be better off dead."

The two men continued to talk idly against the background of activity. Time passed. At twenty minutes past twelve, one of the police officers who had been listening to a continuous stream of information coming in over the short wave radio, suddenly scribbled on a pad and passed the message to Brennan.

"They've found Grisson's car: he's ditched it," Brennan said. "They found it at Pine Hill. Looks like he's taken to the woods." He bent over the map and Fenner, snapping upright, joined him. They studied the map. "Yeah: woods all around here and a couple of farms." He turned to one of his men. "See if you can find out if these two farms are on the telephone. If they are, call them and warn them Grisson might be heading their way."

The police officer grabbed a telephone and dialed information.

After some delay, he reported, "Waite's farm isn't on the telephone: that's the distant one. Hammond's farm is."

"Call Hammond and warn him."

"Can't we go out there now?" Fenner asked. "This sitting around is giving me the ants."

"I have close to two hundred men out there," Brennan said. "What good would we do? As soon as I know where he is holed up—then we'll go."

But it wasn't until five o'clock in the morning as the sun was coming up that the call they were waiting for came through.

The police officer said, "Grisson has been located at Waite's farm, sir," he said, speaking rapidly. "Waite spotted Grisson leaving one of the barns for water ten minutes ago. There's no doubt it's Grisson."

"How about the girl?" Brennan asked, coming over. "Here—give me the phone." He took the receiver. "Chief Brennan here. Let's have it."

"Sergeant Donaghue this end," a voice returned. "No sign of the girl yet, sir. We have the farm completely surrounded. He can't break out. Do we move in and get him?"

"You wait for me," Brennan said. "Kill him if he tries to break out, but otherwise, keep out of sight and wait for me. I'll be with you in under an hour." He slammed down the receiver, saying to the police officer, "Alert that helicopter. I'm on my way." He glanced at Fenner. "Do you want to come with me?"

"I'd like to see you try to stop me," Fenner said and he was first out of the room.

4

Slim woke with a start. His brain became instantly alert. His gun jumped into his hand as he half sat up, blinking in a pale beam of sunlight coming through one of the many chinks in the barn walls. For some moments he couldn't imagine where he was, then he remembered the long walk in the darkness through the woods, seeing the lights of the farmhouse, entering the barn, too weary to go further. He had had trouble in forcing Miss Blandish into the barn. She had been in such an exhausted state she could scarcely walk. He had dragged her up in the loft and pushed her down on the straw covered floor, then he had closed the trap door and had dragged straw across it.

It had been some time before he had fallen asleep. Now as he half sat up, his bones aching from the hard floor, he felt hungry and thirsty. He looked at his watch: it was close to five o'clock. Maybe they would have to stay up in the loft all day. They would have to have water. He looked over at where Miss Blandish lay sleeping, then he pulled aside the straw, opened the trap door and slid quickly down the ladder into the main part of the barn. He went out the door, gun in hand and studied the farmhouse some fifty yards away.

There was no sign of life. Soiled net curtains shielded all the windows. He stood watching for several minutes, then satisfied there was no one up, he moved cautiously into the open.

Old man Waite and his two sons who had been watching from behind the net curtains all night, stiffened at the sight of the tall thin figure in the shabby black suit who came out of the barn, gun in hand.

"That's him," Waite said. "Call the police, Harry. Hurry it up!"

Slim made for the water tank, bucket in hand. He dipped the bucket into the tank, then turning, he hurried back to the barn, unaware that the alarm had gone out and that police cars, packed with armed men, were already on the move towards the isolated farm.

He carried the bucket up into the loft, replaced the trap and set the bucket down. He wished he had been able to get food. He was hungry. He drank some of the water. Then he lay down.

Staring up at the roof of the barn, he tried to make up his mind what he was to do. He was regretting that he had ditched the car, but at the time it seemed the sensible thing to do. Everyone would be on the lookout for the Buick by now. But the long five mile walk through the woods now underlined the fact that he must have a car. Maybe there would, be a car on the farm he could take. He wondered how many people lived in the farmhouse. Maybe, later, they would go out into the fields and give him a chance to steal the car. He closed his eyes. An hour crawled by, and as the minutes passed, the tiny spot of panic in his mind gradually grew. He kept wondering what it would be

like to die. What would happen to him when he was dead? This
was something he couldn't understand. He couldn't believe he
just snuffed out: something must happen to him, he thought,
but what?

He heard Miss Blandish stir and he raised himself up on
his arm. The girl was muttering to herself as she slowly came
awake.

The sound of a distant aircraft came to him only half
consciously as he watched the girl open her eyes.

They looked at each other. He saw her eyes widen and she
shrank back, her hand going to her mouth.

"Don't make a noise!" he snarled. He had an instinctive
feeling that she was about to scream. "Hear me? Don't make a
noise! I'm not coming near you... just stay quiet."

She remained motionless, staring at him as the noise of the
aircraft grew louder and louder and seemed finally to be
immediately over the top of the barn.

Slim's heart suddenly gave a lurch. He realized the
significance of the sound. He scrambled to his feet, pulled aside
the truss of straw and lifted the trap door.

He paused to motion to the girl to stay where she was, then
he slid down the ladder, ran across to the door and peered out.

He was in time to see a helicopter with the white star of the
Army painted on it, settling down in the field at the back of the
farmhouse.

He knew immediately his hiding place had been discovered
and his gun jumped into his hand. He closed the barn door and
dropped the heavy bar into its slot. Through a chink in the door
he peered out into the farmyard.

It wasn't a well-kept farm and there was much litter, two
old tractors, a farm car and a big truck cluttering up the place:
all of which afforded good cover for anyone approaching the
barn.

Suddenly he saw a policeman. The man made a quick,
silent dash from the truck to one of the tractors. He moved so
fast Slim had no time to get his gun up, but it told him as
nothing else could that this was the end of his road.

From behind the shelter of the farmhouse, Brennan and
Fenner climbed out of the helicopter. A big, rubbery-faced police
sergeant and a tall, thin Army Lieutenant greeted them.

"He hasn't broken cover yet, sir," Sergeant Donaghue said. "We've got him trapped. The whole farm is surrounded. This is Lieutenant Hardy."

Brennan shook hands with the Lieutenant.

"Just where is he holed up?" he asked.

"This way, Chief," Donaghue said.

The four men walked across the field to the farmhouse. Brennan noted with approval the circle of armed men, well hidden, lying, rifles in hand, around the perimeter of the farm.

"Careful how you go here, sir," Donaghue said, pausing at the corner of the house. He edged around the side of the house until they could see the farmyard. He pointed to the big barn some fifty yards away. "He's in there."

Brennan studied the ground. The first thirty yards offered excellent cover, but the last twenty yards were bare and open.

"No idea if he has a Thompson, sergeant?"

"No, sir."

"He could do a hell of a lot of damage if he has. Still no sign of the girl?"

"No, sir."

"I'll give him a hail. Got a loudspeaker truck here?"

"It's coming up now, sir."

The men moved back. A few minutes later the loudspeaker truck bumped over the field and pulled up near them. Brennan took the microphone.

"Can you get some of your men behind those two tractors and the truck, Lieutenant?"

"Sure," Hardy said. "I would have got them there before but Donaghue said to wait." He turned to his sergeant and issued orders.

"No shooting," Brennan said. "If the girl's in there we can't take any chances."

"I understand."

Ten soldiers moved quietly out of the cover of the farmhouse. They dropped flat and began to crawl towards the tractors and the truck.

Shaking and sweating, Slim saw them as they crawled out into the open. The khaki uniforms, the steel helmets and the rifles turned him sick with panic. He lifted his gun and tried to get one of the soldiers in his sights, but the gun seemed to be jumping in his hand and snarling with frustrated fear and fury, he fired blindly. He saw the dust kick up about a yard from the nearest soldier who jumped up, bent double, and with two quick strides was behind the truck and out of sight. The other soldiers, also moving with speed, reached their objectives and vanished.

Brennan grunted.

"If he had a Thompson he would have used it," he said to the Lieutenant. "It depends now on how many slugs he's got left. I'll give him a hail." He lifted the microphone. "Grisson! You're surrounded. Come on out with your hands in the air! Grisson! You haven't a chance! Come on out!"

The loud metallic voice echoed in the fresh morning air. Slim listened, his loose mouth closed in a bunched-up mess of wet lips. He yearned for a Thompson gun. He cursed himself for getting trapped like this. He thought of Ma. Pete had said she had fought like a man. He would fight like a man too. He glanced at his gun. He had only five slugs left. Well, he'd take five of the punks with him. They would never get him alive.

Up in the loft, Miss Blandish first heard the shot, then the metallic voice. She realized the moment she had been dreading in a vague, half-conscious way for the past four months was approaching. In a little while she would be free, and the real misery and hell of her experience would begin.

She crawled to the open trap and looked down. She saw Slim standing with his back to her, peering through a chink in the barn door. His thin black back was tense. She saw the gun in his hand. She heard him muttering to himself. There was now silence outside. Her concentrated stare conveyed itself to him.

He turned slowly, and they looked at each other. He, standing by the door, sweating and shaking, and she, lying stretched on the floor, her head and shoulders framed by the trap, looking down at him. They stared at each other for a long time. His face was glistening in the dim light of the barn. His lips came off his teeth and he swore at her, calling her obscene names, hurling them at her in his panic and fear.

She listened, hoping he would eventually shoot her. With all the strength of her mind, she willed him to lift his gun and release a bullet into her, but he did nothing but curse her, glaring at her with his feverish, yellow eyes.

A sound outside made him jerk around. He saw a movement behind the farm cart and he fired. The bang of the gun echoed in the silence. He saw a puff of dust and white splinters of wood fly from the side of the cart.

Once more the loud metallic voice called to him to come out.

"Grisson! We're waiting! You can't get away! Come on out with your hands in the air!"

Panic now flooded his mind. His legs felt weak. His thin wolfish face began to crumple like a child's before it weeps. He slid down on his knees, letting his gun fall to the ground.

Miss Blandish watched him. For a moment she thought he had been shot, but when he began to moan to himself, she drew back, hiding her face in her hands.

Brennan, anxious to get it over, was giving orders to his men. Several soldiers and two police officers got behind the farm cart. Using it as a shield, they began pushing it across the yard towards the barn door.

Slim saw the cart coming. He staggered to his feet, snatched up his gun. In a frenzy of panic and despair, he threw up the bar holding the door in place, dragged open the door and ran out. He fired blindly at the advancing cart, standing in the hot sunshine, his face ghastly with terror.

Two machine guns opened up. Blood suddenly appeared on his dirty white shirt. His gun fell from his hand. The guns stopped as abruptly as they had started.

Brennan and Fenner watched him slowly collapse. His thin legs thrashed for a long moment, jerkily and convulsively, the way a snake dies. His back arched; his hands clawed at the dry dust, then he stiffened and went limp.

The two men, guns in hand, moved across the yard.

Fenner knew before he reached Slim that he was dead. He paused by him for a brief moment. The yellow eyes looked sightlessly up at him. The thin, white, upturned face seemed defenseless and bewildered. The loose mouth hung open. Fenner turned away with a grunt of disgust.

"That's the end of him," Brennan said, "and good riddance."

"Yeah," Fenner said. He drew in a deep breath, then walked slowly towards the barn.

5

Miss Blandish had come down from the loft. The two short bursts of machine gun fire had told her that Grisson was dead. Now, hopelessly, she moved into the darkest part of the barn and sat down on an upturned barrel. She could hear men's voices outside and she flinched from the sound. She dreaded the fast approaching moment when she would have to go out into the hot sunlight and face the curious, staring eyes of her rescuers.

For some moments Fenner didn't see her. He stood in the barn doorway, looking around, and it wasn't until his eyes became accustomed to the shadowy dimness that he did see her. He quickly realized by the tense way she was sitting, how bad this moment must be for her. He moved into the barn and paused when he was some yards from her.

"Hello," he said casually and quietly, "I'm Dave Fenner. Your father asked me to take you home when you are ready to go. There's no rush. You're free now. You tell me what you want to do and I'll fix it."

He saw her relax slightly. He was careful not to approach closer. She reminded him of a cornered, frightened animal, ready to panic at the slightest unexpected movement.

"I thought it might be an idea," he went on, "if I took you to a quiet hotel so you could rest for a while, get a change of clothes and then if you feel like it, to drive you home. I've fixed a room for you at a hotel not far from here. There won't be any fuss. The press don't know anything about this. You won't be bothered. You can go in the back way of the hotel and straight to the room. Would you like to do that?"

She looked intently at him for some moments, then she said "Yes."

"There's a doctor outside," Fenner went on. "He's a nice guy. He wants to meet you. May I bring him in?"

She immediately stiffened, her eyes widening with panic.

"I don't want a doctor!" she said wildly. "What do I want a doctor for? I don't want to see anyone!"

"That's okay," Fenner said. "You don't have to see anyone if you feel that way about it. Will you let me take you to the hotel?"

Again she stared intently at him, hesitating, then she nodded.

"I'll get a car," Fenner said. "You stay right here and don't worry about a thing. You're not going to see anyone. No one's going to bother you."

He turned and walked out of the barn to where Brennan waited. A crowd of soldiers and policemen were staring curiously towards the barn. Old man Waite and his two sons were gaping from the farmhouse door. Four soldiers were carrying Grisson's body to a truck.

As Fenner approached Brennan, the Medical Officer came over. Behind him hovered a nurse.

"She's jumpy," Fenner said. "She doesn't want to see anyone. She doesn't want a doctor. She likes the idea of going to a hotel. She wants me to take her there."

The Medical Officer shrugged his shoulders.

"That's all right," he said. "She must certainly be suffering from shock. It's better to let her do what she wants. I'll go on ahead and fix up a room at the Bonham Hotel. When she's got used to the idea of being free, I'll see her. How about taking the nurse with you?"

"I'd like to," Fenner said, "but I don't think she'd stand for it. She reacted badly when I suggested she should see you."

"Well, all right. I'll get off. I'll have the nurse stand by just in case she's needed. I'll have everything fixed by the time you get her to the hotel. We've got to be sure the press don't get at her. Once this leaks out, they'll be around like a swarm of ants."

"I'll see they don't get near her," Brennan said grimly.

As the Medical Officer hurried away, Fenner said, "Will you get all these men out of the way and leave a car right outside the barn?"

"I'll do it," Brennan said. "You go in there and stay with her."

Fenner waited long enough to see Brennan get rid of the soldiers and the police, then he returned to the barn.

Miss Blandish was still sitting on the upturned barrel. She looked up as he came over to her.

"It's all fixed," he said, taking out a pack of cigarettes. "You have nothing to worry about." He offered a cigarette, and after a moment's hesitation, she took one and accepted the light he held to the cigarette. "Your father thought it would be better to wait at home for you." Fenner went on, lighting a cigarette for himself. "If you want him, I can get him."

Again he saw the panic jump into her eyes.

"I don't want him," she said, not looking at him. "I want to be alone."

"That's okay," Fenner said. "When you want him, he'll be there." He sat down on a bale of straw, some yards from her. "You're probably wondering who I am," he went on, absolutely sure she wasn't wondering anything of the kind, but knowing the necessity of keeping the situation as normal as possible. "I earn a living as a private investigator. Your father came to me..." He went on talking easily and casually, watching, her, seeing at first no interest but as he told her about his life as a newspaperman, about Paula and about some of his cases he saw she was relaxing and after twenty minutes of continuous talking, he saw she was listening. Finally, he decided that the Medical Officer had had time to fix up a room at the hotel and he said, "Well, I don't want to bore you too much about myself. I guess we can go now. You don't have to worry. There's no one outside. Are you ready to go?"

He saw panic once more jump into her eyes, but he got up and went over to the barn door and pulled it wide open. An Oldsmobile stood outside. There was no one in sight.

"It's okay," he said, not looking at her. "Let's go."

He opened the off side door of the car and left it open, then he got in under the driving wheel. He waited. After some minutes, Miss Blandish came slowly and hesitatingly to the barn door. Fenner didn't look at her. She came to the car and got in, slamming the door shut.

Fenner drove down the uneven farm road and onto the dirt road. Miss Blandish sat away from him, staring with great blank eyes in front of her.

It took a little over forty minutes to reach the hotel at Pine Hill. Fenner, who knew the hotel, drove around to the back entrance. There was no one around. He pulled up and got out.

"Wait here. I won't be two seconds," he said and went quickly into the lobby where the Medical Officer was waiting.

"Room 860," he told Fenner, giving him a key. "It's on the top floor. The nurse has got some clothes for her. How is she?"

Fenner shrugged.

"She's not saying much. She's jumpy, but at least she seems to have accepted me. You get out of the way, Doc. I'll take her up."

"See if you can persuade her to see me," the Medical Officer said. "It's important I see her as soon as possible."

"Okay. I'll see what I can do," Fenner said and went back to the car.

Miss Blandish was sitting motionless, looking down at her hands. She glanced up sharply as Fenner came to her. "All ready," he said. "No one to bother you." She got out of the car, and together, they walked into the lobby and entered the elevator.

As they shot to the top floor, she said abruptly, "I heard the shooting. He's dead, isn't he?"

Startled, Fenner said, "Yes. You don't have to think of him any more. That's all behind you."

Neither of them said anything further. He took her along the empty corridor to room 860, unlocked the door and stood aside. She went into the room. The Medical Officer had done a good job. The room was ladened with flowers; there was a wagon of cold food and drinks. The windows stood open and sunlight made patterns on the blue carpet.

Miss Blandish walked slowly over to a big vase of roses. She paused by them, touching the dark scarlet buds. Fenner closed the door.

"Doctor Heath would like to meet you," he said. "Would you mind?"

She looked at him. He was relieved to see there was no panic in her eyes as she said, "I don't want to see anyone yet. There's nothing he can do for me."

"You know what I'd do if I were you?" Fenner said quietly. "I'd take a shower and change out of those clothes. You'll find others in the closet." He opened the closet and took out the clothes the nurse had brought. He handed them to her. "You go ahead and have a shower. I'll wait right here and see no one bothers you. Okay?"

She looked searchingly at him, a puzzled expression in her eyes.

"Do you always treat people like this?" she asked.

"I don't have much chance," Fenner said and smiled. "You go ahead."

She went into the bathroom and shut and locked the door.

Shaking his head, Fenner went over to the window and looked down at the slow-moving traffic far below. The cars looked like toys. Immediately below, outside the entrance to the hotel, he saw a group of men, several with cameras and flashguns, arguing with three policemen who guarded the entrance. So the news had leaked out, he thought. Now there would be trouble. In a little while the town would be swarming with newspapermen.

He turned away from the window and went to the door, looking out into the passage. Three policemen lounged at the head of the stairs. Brennan had said he would keep the press away from the girl: he was carrying out his promise, but Fenner knew sooner or later when they took her from the hotel, the press would close in on her like a pack of jackals.

A quarter of an hour later, the bathroom door opened and Miss Blandish came out. She had changed into the flowered dress the nurse had bought and it suited her.

Fenner thought he had never seen a girl so beautiful.

"I bet you feel all the better for that, don't you?" he said.

She moved to the window before he could stop her and looked out. She moved quickly back, turning to face him, her eyes frightened.

"It's all right," he said soothingly. "You don't have to worry. They won't come up here. Look, sit down and relax. Don't you want something to eat?"

"No." She sat down, putting her hands to her face.

He watched her during a long, uneasy pause, then she said suddenly, her tone desperate, "I don't know what I'm going to do."

"Don't think about it now," Fenner said gently. "You'll find it will work out. People forget. It'll be tough going for the first three or four days, then they'll forget about you. Right now what you've gone through is in focus, but after a while, it'll get out of focus and later on, even you'll forget about it. You're young. You have lots of things to look forward to." He was talking for the sake of talking: feeling he had to say something. He didn't believe what he was saying. He was sure she didn't either.

"You said he was dead, but he isn't." She shivered. "He is with me now." She made a helpless gesture. "I don't know what my father will say. At first I thought it couldn't have happened to me, but now I know it has. I just don't know what I'm going to do!"

Fenner felt a cold sweat on his face. This was a complication he hadn't expected nor even dreamed of: a situation he felt incompetent to handle.

"Wouldn't it be an idea to send for your father?" he said uneasily. "You can't cope with a thing like this on your own. Let me send for him."

She shook her head.

"No." She looked up. Her eyes were like holes cut in a white sheet. "He wouldn't be able to help me. He would just be horribly embarrassed and upset. This is something I should be able to work out for myself, but the trouble is I'm not fitted to cope with any major crisis in my life. I have never had any reason to cope with anything. I have never had any sense of values. I've just enjoyed a good time all the time until this happened. I suppose it is a test for me, isn't it? But instead of a test, I feel it is a trap. I don't know if I'm capable of getting out of it. I'm ashamed of myself. I'm a person without any background, any character or any faith. Some people could cope with this because they believe in God. I haven't believed in anything except having a good time." She clenched and unclenched her fists, then she looked up; her fixed smile made Fenner feel bad. "Perhaps I had better see the doctor. He will give me something. Then, as you said, in a few days' time, I'll be able to face this thing." She looked away and went on as if speaking to herself, "You see how weak I am. I have to have someone to lean on. I haven't the equipment to rely on myself. It's because I have been brought up to rely on other people, but it is my fault. I'm not blaming anyone but myself."

"I'll get him," Fenner said. "You mustn't be hard on yourself. You'll get over it. You must expect to have to rely on someone at first after what you've gone through. You're going to be all right. You've just got to hang on for the next few days."

Her smile became a grimace.

"Would you hurry, please?" she said politely. "I must have something. He'll know what to give me. I shall go to pieces if I don't get something. I have been living on drugs now for months."

"I'll get him," Fenner said and went quickly to the door. Leaving it open, he stepped into the passage and called to one of the policemen. "Hey, you! Get the Doc up here, will you, and fast?"

The door slammed behind him, making him spin around. He heard the lock snap to.

In a sudden panic, he rapped on the door, but Miss Blandish didn't open the door. He drew back and drove his shoulder against the door panel, but the door didn't give.

The two policemen ran up.

"Get it open!" Fenner shouted, feeling sweat on his face. "Hurry!"

As the two policemen's combined weight smashed open the door, Fenner heard a thin, wailing scream. It sounded far away.

From the street below, he heard people shouting and the sound of traffic grinding to a stop.

He stood helplessly in the doorway and looked around the empty room.

Printed in September 2021
by Rotomail Italia S.p.A., Vignate (MI) - Italy